DOG SYMPHONY

Sam Munson

DOG SYMPHONY

A NEW DIRECTIONS
PAPERBOOK ORIGINAL

Manufactured in the United States of America
New Directions Books are printed on acid-free paper
First published in 2018 as New Directions Paperbook 1415

Library of Congress Cataloging-in-Publication Data
Names: Munson, Sam, author.
Title: Dog symphony / by Sam Munson.
Description: First edition. | New York : New Directions Books, 2018. |
"A New Directions Paperbook."
Identifiers: LCCN 2018009878 (print) | LCCN 2018002152 (ebook) |
ISBN 9780811227698 (ebook) | ISBN 9780811227681 (alk. paper)
Classification: LCC PS3613.U6936 (print) | LCC PS3613.U6936 D64 2018 (ebook) |
DDC 813/.6—dc23

2 4 6 8 10 9 7 5 3 1

New Directions Books are published for James Laughlin
by New Directions Publishing Corporation
80 Eighth Avenue, New York 10011

God, *de potentia absoluta*, is infinitely everything, infinitely good, bad, just, unjust, compassionate, cruel, stupid, etc., etc....

—CAMILO JOSÉ CELA
SAN CAMILO, 1936

DOG SYMPHONY

1.

HUMANS SUFFER AS DOGS suffer, they struggle as dogs struggle, they love order as dogs love order. Long live the whistle and baton.

I came to Argentina at the invitation of Dr. Ana Mariategui. I had known her, at that point, for nine years. She started her academic career at the University of Santiago; the University of Buenos Aires recruited her two years prior to our first meeting. We worked in a minuscule field. I studied the history of prison architecture. She was, in turn, a historiographer of the technical jargon that prison historians use in their profession.

We had often spoken of visiting each other. I will come to you, she said, and you can show me the sights of the northern capital (her private name for my city); you can come to me, and I will show you the sights of this shithole. I did not use those terms to describe Buenos Aires; in our correspondence I referred to it only as the southern capital. This dilatory premise we conceived and resuscitated many times through our near decade of friendship, but nothing ever came of it. We always met in cities foreign to us both. Prague, where we became acquainted; Lyon, where we slept together for the first time; Austin, Texas, where I was extremely sick and Ana read aloud to me from *Dead*

Souls, which she always carried with her on her travels, along with the *Pensées*; Istanbul, where we got lost in Kasımpaşa by becoming too drunk to follow our guide's directions and had to present ourselves at a local police precinct. The sergeant there knew—miraculously—the name of the tour company our academic sponsors had hired, who saved us by shouting into the void through an old, grass-green walkie-talkie. Milan, where we were captured with a third colleague—whose name we could never remember—on a slanted rock near a palazzo (pink, like a urinal cake) in a photograph I kept in my wallet to savor its spectacular compositional failure. I have my back to the camera. Cigarette smoke floats in a ribbon away from my head. Ana's arms are crossed under her breasts, her signal gesture meaning: fuck off, enough. Our anonymous, balding, fox-faced fellow scholar stands atop the rock with his abdomen thrust forward and covered by an orange vest. He resembling a wooden figurine of V. I. Lenin.

Ana's invitation to Buenos Aires thus surprised me. I read it in the hallway outside my apartment door, in the deadened, ticket-of-leave light. The University planned to hold a conference, she wrote, and she was confident she could get me invited. Its architect a new eminence, a man named Sanchis Mira. She knew little about him, except that he had once been a professor of French but now worked in an interdisciplinary field: sociology, politics, law—three streams of shit, Boris Leonidovich, flowing and joining together, she wrote, but if you come, you will at last see for yourself the world's asshole, the true *anus mundi*. I wrote back the next day, accepting her pseudoinvitation. I was delighted to do so, for (*contra* Seneca) we all lose ourselves when we travel, our personalities such as they may be collapse into generalized behavior, and I was curious, most curious, to see this unusual woman at home. In due course (as they say) my official conference invitation arrived, a thick blue-and-white envelope, containing a program of events and a brochure with information about the University. My name appeared on the program with Ana's. We would be presenting together. A coincidence she must have arranged, I thought.

I planned to use the conference to workshop a paper on the innovations that marked out the Butyrka Prison in Moscow as singular, innovations developed during its original construction in the late eighteenth century. I had spent the winter teaching a course on Russia's prisons, a dubious process I kept Ana informed of through my letters. My lectures, in general, were well attended because I gave high grades to all my students in order to save myself effort. I gave exams and assigned papers, but I did not read the resulting work. I merely ran my eyes over the answers, the paragraphs, the cenotaphic bibliographies, and graded them A, or A minus at worst. As a result, my classes conducted themselves. The students were happy and I was happy. The students had all the freedom they needed to practice their unending moronism, which is, let me add, the inalienable and universal right of students. I remained free to practice my scholarly moronism—the status of that right being far more ambiguous. Ana was sympathetic, yet she understood, she wrote, that despite my cynical praise for student moronism, it might be hindering me. All the more reason to attend this conference. You will never amount to anything, she wrote, if you keep yourself mired at all times in student moronism. The word *mired* she surrounded, as was her habit, with a fine, miniaturized drawing for emphasis: a small human figure sinking beneath sharp waves (these resembled the teeth of an animal). The letter contained nothing out of the ordinary. Her prose was ruthless as always, and her handwriting hasty. It worried me all the same. The sarcasm she habitually employed in discussing her work was largely absent from the letter, a sign (I suspected) of anxiety or another unmentioned suffering. I dismissed this as a romantic fantasy and did not mention it to her in my reply. Such concerns are for a husband to worry about, and we did not engage in domestic theater. In her next letter, her sarcasm was restored, at least partially: she wrote that the University is an old whore but its students are not even the progeny of this whore—they are the progeny of a whore's ideals, phantasms, burgherly poltergeists.

This remarkable phrase arrived the day it first snowed. Soft, ragged flakes scraped my kitchen window, glaucous in the late morning light. The snowfall continued all day and into the night, through my invigilation of the final exam. My class comprised three human elements. Two student armies, one slightly larger and slightly stupider and one slightly smaller and slightly more intelligent. But in truth the conscripts mustered for each could have served equally well the other faction. And in truth intellect and stupidity remain indistinguishable. I remember them chiefly as a collection of clear, darting eyes and dark mouths. A married couple in late middle age formed the third element, the Zygmunds. Both red-cheeked and childishly excitable, their scalps covered with white, loose, flame-like hair. The student armies had adopted them as shared mascots. The Zygmunds served unwittingly in this capacity. They always sat far in the back, behind the stupidest tier of the stupider army (the armies arranged themselves more or less in order of "intellectual ability") and did not say much, but their written work attained a high, even youthful standard of excellence. They themselves had both worked as chemistry professors; in their retirement, they had decided to study history, a private passion of theirs. After the exam, the smaller, less stupid army demanded that we go as a class to a bar to celebrate our liberation, as they called it. The stupider army acceded to this demand, and the Zygmunds came too. We marched across the blanketed grass of the quadrangle and across the avenue gleaming a black gleam from melted snow. The notice boards we passed on the way all held posters for a play being put on, one I'd never heard of: *Canis Major*. Both student armies began to bark in honor of this at the huge, chalky moon.

I spoke to no one beside the Zygmunds during this excursion. The student armies dissolved as soon as we entered the bar, but the barking and baying continued in erratic bursts. I sat with the Zygmunds, their eyes and white hair blazing in the improvised and fleet light of the bar, candlelight, firelight, light of civilization. The crepuscular, yellow, orange, oblong, virtuoso, unimprovable, unitary, meridional glow. What you can accomplish in the so-called light of civilization defies definition, I thought. They asked me what my plans for the break were, and I told them I was bound for Buenos Aires, for an academic conference. Mr. Zygmund said, without hesitating, that I must stay with their daughter—she lives in Flores, a truly excellent neighborhood! I refused, saying I could not possibly impose. Mrs. Zygmund, flushed with embarrassment on my behalf, said that they had meant as a paying guest. Their daughter owned and operated, they said, a small hotel. A pension, in fact, called the Pensión Vermesser. They assured me that the hotel was excellent, and I raised my glass to them in a silent valediction.

I left soon after, walking to my apartment through the thickening snowfall, which had covered the streets and pavements in a fragile, half-luminous sheet. My boots left small voids, and more snow quickly effaced them. When I got home, my phone was ringing, though it was well after midnight. I heard it from the hallway; somehow it was apparent at once that it had been ringing for hours. The ringing continued as I took off my coat and kicked the snow from my boots; it shrilled as I passed the mirror, which showed me—as always—my dark receded hair, my crude jaw, my nostril flesh beset with blackheads, a greasy, cold-reddened ear. No one answered my greeting. I thought I heard a quiet breath, or a sob, or a choked laugh, amid all the hissing emptiness, the true sound of phenomenal existence. I listened. I cried out another hello. Then I hung up.

2.

OUR ARRIVAL WAS SEVERELY delayed. We sat on the tarmac
at Pistarini International Airport for one hour, which turned
into another. The captain said, again and again, in his murky
voice, that we would soon be at our gate. Each time he was
proven wrong. The ventilation system filled the stifling cabin
with a white roar. Loud complaints kept erupting ahead of me,
behind me, to my right. Fuck this, we paid our money, stop
fucking around. Among these complaints was another, one that
made no sense. It's those useless fuckers from the department,
whispered the seam-faced old woman across the aisle. The man
to her right hushed her. Don't get so upset, he said, it might be
them but there's no point in causing trouble. Close to midnight,
we began to taxi toward what the captain promised was our
gate. His voice woke me from a dream of Ana, a dream based
on the photograph from Milan (I knew this even as I dreamed
the dream). Our Lenin-like colleague ran around on all fours
while Ana stood on the rock. I was nowhere to be seen. A storm
floated leadenly above Lake Como, and the pink palazzo was
consumed and left standing as though by invisible flames.

Before I went to the customs line, before I urinated, I located
a payphone and called Ana's office number. The airport air was
cold and sweet, like the melancholy (I assumed) that overtook

its namesake during his exile in Tierra del Fuego. I knew there was little chance Ana would be in her office this late, but I had to try. The line bleated. No one answered. I tried again; still nothing. I was disappointed. I had never been to Buenos Aires. In fact it was my first time in the southern hemisphere, and Ana was my sole acquaintance in the southern capital. We hadn't made any firm plans to meet on the night of my arrival, but I had hoped to see her. My address book was buried at the bottom of my suitcase, and I did not want to paw through my shirts and my papers to reach it. In any case I knew my destination. Before my departure, the Zygmunds had assured me their daughter had an empty room, and had even arranged for her to give me a special rate. The Pensión Vermesser was located, as they had said, in Flores, on José Bonifacio. I surveyed the maps of public transit. I could have gotten there on the Subte, or by taking a long bus ride, but my suitcase was too heavy. I had brought two enormous reference works, Chulkov's *Toward a General Theory* and Apukhtin's monumental work on shackling. (As my suitcase creaked I envied Ana: the *Pensées* and *Dead Souls* take up almost no space, being books of pure void.)

Few other travelers filled the concourse as I headed for the customs line. Not even the tired and furious people I had deplaned with could be seen. The only other human beings, in fact, were four men in sky-blue uniforms, strolling along the wide path between the seating areas for the gates. I did not recognize their uniform markings. As a result of my studies, I was well acquainted with police and corrections uniforms from around the world, but their sky-blue liveries seemed completely new, completely alien. Above their stiff collars floated the jovial, slightly sly communal expression you often see on state-owned faces. One man carried a shovel over his shoulder. Grayish crusts of earth clung to the bright blade. Five more in sky-blue uniforms gathered near the customs line where I stood waiting my turn to approach the bored-looking officer in his hexagonal glass booth. He, at least, wore the familiar uniform of the Argentine customs police—a dim, dusty blue. He stamped my passport. I asked him about the strangely dressed security officers, and he shrugged. To be honest, sir, I can't tell you exactly what they do here, he muttered. At the taxi line, another contingent in sky blue (much smaller, only two members) hovered near the line's head, holding clipboards. I ducked into my taxi and gave my destination. My driver grunted. The two officers made quick, spastic notes. As we drove past them they smiled equilateral and enameled smiles. I asked my driver what agency they represented, but he didn't respond. His nape, raw pink and carbuncular, floated ahead of me in the dimness.

At the Pensión Vermesser, the Zygmunds' daughter Violeta came out to welcome me despite the time. Watch your step, she shouted as I got out of the taxi. I almost tripped over two large stainless-steel bowls—fresh, red slabs of meat lay in one and clear water filled the other—near the brief limestone staircase that led up to her bluish doorway. The steps glowed, more or less, in the moonlight. Inside the pension, pale oblong shapes decorated the white parlor walls, left—I assumed—by taken-down pictures. Violeta swept a strong-looking hand through air as she guided me deeper into the pension. I am having everything reframed, she explained. A woman my age cannot allow student framing efforts to deface her walls. From the silent floor rose a harsh, addictive smell—wood polish. I recognized it at once. The smell permeated my room as well. Four right angles, one window overlooking the street, an oak bedstead, the carved footboard displaying two bas-relief whippets curled in sleep. A Formica desk mimicked the oak. Through a narrow doorway the hard yellow bathroom tile glared its dental glare. A fly darted in and out of the milk-glass bathroom window louvers. Up close, a fly's head resembles a ceremonial mace covered in verdigris—that's a fact. But I merely observed from a distance.

Violeta told me I was free to do as I liked, but that I must make sure to bring my three keys—to the gate, the front door, and this bedroom—with me if I planned to go out. She required massive doses of barbiturates to sleep and would not, she assured me, awake to let me in no matter how loudly I yelled or rang the buzzer. The absence of other guests meant I was on my own. I thanked her for the warning and asked if Dr. Mariategui had called. That's an unusual name, said Violeta. I know only one Mariategui and he too is a doctor, he's a nephrologist in Colegiales. But no, I've gotten no calls today. None at all. I run a quiet house. Quiet is essential. My mother and father tell me you're a writer and thinker. So I'm sure you will agree.

It was now far too late to call Ana at home. I decided instead to revise the paper I planned to present at the conference. I laid out my typescript and the reference works I'd brought with me and uncapped my two plastic pens, one green and one blue. As soon as I sat down to work, however, a sudden nausea beset me. I have always hated my profession. Yet I could, I admit, follow no other. Each time I traveled this hatred hardened and worsened. I tried to emend the first paragraph, but found myself on my feet, unpacking my shirts. My last name inked into the collars: Pasternak. No relation to the poet, novelist, and correspondent with Rilke. My namesake never packed or unpacked anything, he had servants. And Rilke wore the same shirt at all times to express his fake poverty and material indifference. I sat down at the desk again, but it was no use. My handwriting crawled across the typed pages, useless and smeared. My head began to throb. I poured cold water onto my hair and face and I changed my socks. I decided to take a long (and mendacious) walk. On my way out, I grabbed my gray jacket and shook it. A heavy metallic chord sounded. This was my shorthand method of checking to see if the jacket contained my keys, a method I had developed in my own apartment. It had never failed me. Below my feet the rooms and corridors of the pension extended left and right, and beyond them, as noted, nocturnal affairs, nocturnal matters and events, stars or their absence, qualia in that family. In the living room, a mouse waited under the piano. (For what?)

I walked along without heed. I have a natural talent for memorizing maps and plans. I believe this is what led me to my profession. All serious students of prison architecture must possess this facility. For weeks prior to my trip I had memorized maps of Buenos Aires. This pathological habit now meant that I felt totally secure in my wanderings, totally secure in my arbitrary decision to head east on José Bonifacio. (And as far as the so-called Spanish language is concerned, I have always spoken it fluently.) At regular intervals along the sidewalk, thin poplar trees pointed upward into the night. The pavement gave up the warmth it had accumulated during the day. After twenty minutes of this heedless walking, I read the street-sign plaque on the nearest building to check my progress. The deep blue plaque, covered with the bitter shine of fired enamel, displayed the simple, lyrical name: Camacuá. That's where I stood. North of Directorio and the Plaza de la Misericordia. An enormous, crooked eucalyptus tree creaked next to a gabled house with its windows boarded. A quiet, enleafed intersection, nothing much. The air damp and warmish. Through it the drilling whines of mosquitoes passed like current. I missed Ana. In fact, the expression "drilling whines of mosquitoes passed like current" I had stolen from her. Her letters contained numerous rich phrases alongside her lacerating sarcasm. Had she been present, I thought, she could have explained this gabled house or provided a vicious and satirical history of its inhabitants. Though she had lived in Buenos Aires for more than a decade, she regarded almost all Argentines as cryptofascists.

If I kept following Bonifacio east it would end at La Plata, but in that case I could proceed along Carlos Calvo across the river and into the dark Reserva Ecológica, beyond which lay the Atlantic. At the ocean's edge, the nature preserve breathed, three rough lobes. Lautaro was the next street east, and I could see in the humid night the blue flame of its street sign. After Lautaro would come Carabobo, Pumacahua, Curapaligüé, and Thorne, which took its name from Juan Bautista Thorne, a naval fighter in the wars of the Rosas regime born in my own natal city but to Argentine parents.

The streetlamps hummed in dignified terror. A bullmastiff, night-colored and sleek, slid from behind a red, rusted, cylindrical mailbox and trotted across my path. Some corpuscles slipped through my heart and lungs.

3.

THIS WAS HOW I discovered my error: I thrust my hand automatically into my pocket to fondle the pension keys, and found that coins, centavos, had made the heavy chord I'd heard after shaking my jacket. Now I truly missed Ana. Had it not been so late, I would have tried to track her down and visit her at her apartment, which I had never seen. Instead, I counted the money I had on me—enough to pay for a cheap hotel, I projected, a place where you rented rooms by the hour. I decided to find one, sleep, and head back to the pension after Violeta's barbiturate trance had come to an end, which I guessed would be sometime before nine so that she could attend to her guests.

I walked on Mitre all the way to Hualfin without seeing another fellow ambler. On the northeast corner, grayish light poured through the windows of a small, coffin-shaped all-night store. Two bowls glimmered near its door, just like those I'd seen at the pension. One filled with cloudy water and one with a black mass whose stench I could detect even from afar. As I got closer I saw the bowl held putrefied, almost liquefied meat. It made me hesitate before entering but I had no choice, I needed cigarettes. And the store itself, well, there was nothing else unusual about it. A radio paneled in artificial pine played a wild, repetitive song at an almost inaudible volume. No words, just hoarse cries, drumbeats, and bells. Surrounded by the gentle, raucous noise, I purchased a pack of Macedonias, a brand I had never smoked, and the clerk blinked morosely at me as he tendered my change. As though he were trying to remember where he had seen me before. Or perhaps he simply wanted to show me the expressive gaze of defeat. In either case a mild, murky benevolence shone (as they say) from his eyes. I wanted to ask him about the water and rotten meat. The possible explanations I formulated—that he was insane or mourning a lost pet—advised silence. Though I did ask him if he knew anyplace cheap to stay that would take a latecomer. He shook his head no. A white dog, a Samoyed, trotted up to the shop doorway and stuck its head through. The clerk's quiescent, forlorn face opened as the dog drooled. It watched the rotten meat in the steel bowl, and it nosed the water. Then it trotted away without eating or drinking. The fur around its paws stained by anonymous filth. The clerk shrugged. The night sighed on his behalf.

Humid quiet extended from street to street, from avenue to avenue. And the boulevards? Also the boulevards. Burgher adventurism proclaims: foreign localities. And further: aesthetic perfection. If you amble through nocturnal streets, truth or some similar defecated ideal will rise from the sewers or rain from the heavens. I don't know about all that, but I do know that the air of Caballito was mild and the air of Balvanera was milder. As a result I did not suffer during my aimless walk. Whenever I tired myself out I sat down on a bench or some cement stairs to rest. No one interfered with me. I saw no fellow Homo sapiens other than the clerk. I continued submerged in this night, accompanied by a wedge of dogs. Not strays—they wore collars and tags and displayed the slick, warm-looking pelts of domestic animals, like the one I'd seen slipping from behind the red mailbox. The lead dog, the point, so to speak, was a smoke-gray Great Dane with docked ears (shaped like hatchet blades). His head was almost as high as a parking meter he passed. His subaltern dogs (I counted six) kept formation in perfect silence, except for the harmonic jingling of their tags. They followed me— or I followed them—northeast along Morón where, in front of every doorway, commercial or residential, I saw the same two objects: metal bowls. One filled with water and the other with meat. In most cases the deep pink of muscle, but also present were organ meats. Luminous and concentrated darkness. The wandering dogs stopped to eat and drink in regal quiet. Their syncopated lapping rippled through the night. They did not fight over the meat but ate as interior ministers might eat with grave calculation. At certain doorways the meat had been left out and ignored by the dogs long enough to start rotting, to have drawn a wriggling coat of flies, to emit a stink I could detect from far away, like the meat in the all-night store's bowl.

The pack of seven did not follow any apparent system in choosing which bowls to eat and drink from. The subalterns broke ranks before visiting a bowl and rejoined them after they had finished. At Nazca, I—or rather, we—encountered another, much larger pack. Twenty-eight or twenty-nine dogs at least, all proceeding in the same ministerial silence and equanimity. The wedge was absorbed and assimilated by this larger pack. My innate suspicion of dogs hindered me here. The sheer number pacing along Nazca, the absence of human authorities—all in all it looked like a murky situation, one I did not want to plunge more deeply into, except I did, I did, some yellowed nullity or something like that drove me on to Nazca, among the gathering dogs. All sizes and breeds, they walked or cantered, each dog might itself have been alone, and I might have been alone, except for the stale canine smell that tainted the air above Nazca and above Juan B. Justo, where the number of dogs swelled, by my quick, awed count, into the hundreds without any of the violent sporting common when dogs meet.

No, these dogs trotted with their eyes on the sidewalks, their black eyes or their blue eyes, and I moved among them, keeping to the sidewalk when I could. Sometimes the mass and volume of the dogs forced me to move all the way into the middle of the street, where I walked along the leprous and human lines of paint on the asphalt. The stale smell grew stronger and stronger, it's true, but the night kept on accommodating it, as it accommodated the baleful light from the streetlamps—as well as my own visions of Ana asleep alone. At Condarco, I stumbled over a curb and stepped on the left forepaw of a golden retriever. The dog whined but did not spare me another glance. My terror receded. Gavilán disgorged six identical British bulldogs in identical steel-studded collars, a truly ministerial sight. We reached Donato Álvarez and the stream of dogs from Justo expanded into a river. Turbid and slow, to extend the metaphor, although a river made up entirely of dogs is nonsensical. The only physical phenomenon it bore any resemblance to was a colloidal suspension. Or better still, blood cells in a vein, discrete entities in an environment, phenomena bathed in concepts. That's what filled Donato Álvarez, northwest and southeast, the dual prospect writhing, mighty, indisputable.

Our apparent destination: Chacarita. I knew nothing about that barrio, beyond the name and precise location of all the streets it contained, and that it was once a collection of small farms owned by the Jesuits, and that it took its name from the mightiest and most perfect cemetery in the city (or vice versa). Between Diáz and Cervantes (not named after the author of the Quixote but another Cervantes) we passed a huge, salmon-pink apartment block set back from the street by a clean, fenced, curving driveway. At either end of this driveway, metal-roofed shelters—guard booths, both filled with yellow light—gleamed above the meat and water bowls. The northwestern bowl filled with fresh meat and the southeastern with rotting meat. The dogs preferred the fresher bowl, soon emptying it. They ignored the rotten meat, contrary to what I knew about the nature of dogs. Like human nature, dog nature will approve the consumption of any filth as long as it is present.

The private homes on this block and the next all had wooden shrines out front, carved with motionless leaves and looking as though the same hands had built them. At the apex of a small green triangle jutting out into the intersection where Donato Álvarez met García and Espinosa, the dogs formed a semiorderly knot around a cupola in which an uncertain light flickered. A crimson glass hurricane lamp.

I thought it likely that the dogs, after reaching Warnes, would head over to Newbery and then turn onto Guzmán to reach the main cemetery entrance with its mighty colonnade shining (as they say) in the moonlight, in the metaphorical moonlight. I'd never seen the entrance, but I knew it from the photos in my atlases and city guidebooks. I knew the layout with such precision that I could mentally count the involutes in the shadow cast by the iron cemetery gate. Warnes spread before us, and the press of dogs, their strong smell—mingled now with a harsher odor rising from the ramifying rivulets of dog piss—grew closer, more adherent. The body shops and auto-parts stores lining the blocks of Warnes between Trelles and Oroño proffered the richest meat-bowl displays yet, displays truly commensurate with a rigorous commercial life. Light-streaked chrome bulged behind windows under awnings made of the pollen-yellow canvas that auto-parts stores favor around the world. Grimy steel security lattices screened the doors of these shops, and the bowl shrines before them put the other ones I had seen to shame. The store owners made use of the local elements, i.e., hubcaps, raw sheet-metal plaques for spot welding, and mirror fragments. You could tell owners had made these shrines. The care visible in their construction proved they were not the work of mere lackeys. The mightiest shrine dominated the intersection of Warnes and Dickman, a ziggurat walled with corrugated iron shingling and encircled, netted, in fine-linked drive chains of galvanized steel. The mild wind moaned as it passed through this structure, and I stopped walking in order to listen, though my companions just went on trooping, increasing their numbers, went on flowing. From the ziggurat roof a hood ornament, quite new and greasy, protruded. A naked young woman bent backward by ecstasy, by the wind. No nipples, no genitals, smooth thighs and smooth eyes.

There were no cars on Warnes, and the railway tracks between the street and the southern wall of the cemetery threw off implacable gleams. Toward these implacable gleams, across the asphalt and then the tracks, the dogs trooped without fear. Not toward the entrance on Guzmán. No, they headed instead for a point in the cemetery's outer wall directly across Warnes from Almirante Seguí, Francisco José, another naval mastermind, I thought—his face, surmounted by an absurd Napoleonic curl, appeared in the city atlas I'd studied before coming. Around this inexplicable point their congregation was thickest and most active, nails scraping runnels, for example, in the narrow strip of bare earth between the cemetery and tracks, bare earth also occupied in absorbing urine and slaver.

The wall itself, I saw, that was their aim. The wall that (in the stupidest way possible) separates the living from the dead. No burgher can resist a cemetery wall, so I pressed forward among the knee-high and supernally polite masses. Their pelts stroked my shins. At times a tongue brushed me, or even a tooth, with no intent. I reached the bare verge and struck with my toes a dull, hard blow against a rail hiding itself in the canine darkness before the dogs' true goal became apparent. Their polite writhing expressed a single purpose: to struggle through a break in the cemetery wall shaped like an onion dome. (*Lukovichnaya glava* to my namesake, though in my profession the phrase means "toilet bowl.") Here, any observer would expect their calm to erupt, here—here and nowhere else would they reveal their true nature. Yet sedate motion reigned, the diffuse, sickly light from the streetlamps flowed peaceably on, and the silence did not suffer. Not at all.

The lawns beyond the wall looked almost black in the moonlight. The stone monuments gave off a gentle and mycoform effulgence. Every time I tried to get through this gap—the sweet, wide, and somber lawns of the cemetery were calling me onward—I failed. The dogs congregated too thickly. While they had so far ignored me, I did not want to offend or provoke them. So I gave up, that's all. I crossed the bare verge now moistened by urine; I crossed the train tracks now thrumming, mildly thrumming; I followed the cemetery wall along Warnes and turned on Newbery, where a massive bank of sycamore screened both the cemetery and its brown wall from view. I planned to pass through the mighty colonnade, to climb over the iron gate if necessary. Those involutes twisted and swayed in the night, and I would climb them, I would ascend. To what? To the cemetery. If it is permissible to say "ascend to the cemetery." It seemed an ideal place to spend the night, walled and containing only the dead and these calm dogs. My absorption in the night-dog phenomenon meant I had not yet found an open hotel or flophouse. I did not know what the penal statutes dealing with cemetery trespass demanded in Buenos Aires. In my most recent survey of their crime statistics I had not found one mention of cemetery trespass, and the statutes governing it had evaded my research.

I decided that if I was caught by a night watchman I would tell him I was a "writer." (NB: the generalized "writer" does not exist; all real talent clings to specific forms.) I would explain to this theoretical watchman that spending a night in La Chacarita was essential to my "writing." I found a pen in my jacket pocket: that's proof. Also a folded paper scrap in my wallet, on which I wrote down the words *oak upright, night, canine might, hubcap manufacturer's delight*. The fetus of a poem: more proof. The dogs now trotted with increased, almost desperate speed down Newbery as I jogged up it, and even the ones urinating or defecating did so in a human hurry. I'd never seen anything like it before. Dogs always take their time shitting and pissing and here they were, shitting and pissing on the run, their quiet howls less frequent. Fewer galloped past now, unhappy stragglers heading for the gap in the cemetery wall. The moon was down. The first livid tints of the sunrise stained the sky. The long streets that led to the ocean began to reveal themselves.

No police or cemetery watchmen in the entrance plaza, only two periwinkle nylon tents fronted by crude wooden counters, facing each other with martial indifference. The last dogs ran past, real blurs, yowling and barking, ragged echoes multiplying, and I lay full-length on a cool, whitish bench. I closed my eyes. I listened to the rapid rustling of the nylon and the rarer and rarer shouts from the dogs as the air warmed around me. In short, I passed out at the foot of my goal. And that's how I knew I was still human.

4.

THE MURMURS OF TWO flower vendors mingled in the stagnant heat. The vendors occupied the two tents. They shared one skinny lackey, a teenaged boy with no shirt, who darted back and forth between the tents spraying water on the flowers from a plastic bottle, adjusting their blossoms, repositioning their stems in their green buckets, and muttering to his two masters.

Southern sunlight coated the white marble entrance plaza, the flagstones, and the benches. Like incipient blindness. When I staggered into the shade of the blue-lipped tent roof, I found relief, though the pollen-thickened air was hard to breathe. The lilies and freesia crammed into the buckets emitted their suffocating and meretricious (in the literal sense) smell. Green, raw-looking shelves above and behind the green buckets held a small variety of other goods: cigarettes, gum, plastic combs, antacid tablets, bottled water, fringed leather key-ring fobs to which gold-leaf labels reading (in English) GENUINE PAMPAS HARE had been affixed. I bought a bottle of water so I would have an excuse to speak to the vendor, ask him what time it was and if he had any matches. I had not put my wristwatch on before my walk and had exhausted the matchbook the sad clerk had given me. I thought you were going to ask me for a beer, said the vendor, you look like a derelict. Pollen speckled his iron-colored hair. We don't sell any, he went on, but maybe we should. I said that I never knew anyone to lose money selling beer. The vendor told me my Spanish was good, so good he didn't believe I was a tourist. And I know you're not from Uruguay, you're too tall, he said. I didn't see any other customers, and the vendor must have noticed me noticing, because he spoke up: We don't get a lot of customers at this time of day, but we stay open anyway. His counterpart cried out that they had to, you never knew what was going to happen, what if someone showed up to visit a relative and we weren't here to sell them flowers?

They were brothers, it turned out. The Taquini brothers. They had operated the stands for eleven years, said Fulvio (the elder, who sold me the water), eleven good years. The water worsened my headache but cooled my throat, so I kept drinking and drinking, while glancing around to see if the dogs were present, asleep in the humble (even humiliating) shadows dogs like. I saw none. I asked Fulvio where they'd gone. He looked off into the stony glare beyond the tent, and I repeated my question. What dogs, said Fulvio.

I began to stammer, to wonder if I had dreamed up the quiet, orderly animals that filled the southern night. But Fulvio's brother shouted: Stop fucking with him. Fulvio grinned, tight and dull—except for his golden incisor. The dogs, where do I start, he sighed. Fuckers, shouted Adriano, you have to say they're fuckers before you can say anything else, otherwise you won't convey the truth. Fulvio, peeping through his thick fingers, told me that their arrival had hurt the business. The lull he had blamed on the hour was merely one more vacuity in their empty days, their empty months; Adriano added that at first the dogs hadn't done them any harm, that people still came to visit their dead parents and siblings, they still bought flowers, and still tended the grass on their graves, but that after two weeks or maybe three, the pedestrian traffic slowed and the only visitors who still showed up came from outside the city, where the dogs had not yet spread. You don't know that, said Fulvio, my friend in Coronel Pringles said there'd been sightings of at least a few dogs at night there, and people have started putting out meat and water. Worse, said Fulvio, his friend had even seen a shrine go up. That's when we knew we were in trouble, said Adriano, when we saw the first shrine. I told you—right, Fulvio? It was about two months ago, and business really fell off after that. I asked them why the dogs had done so much damage, if the locals thought the cemetery was unsafe because of them. Adriano said, amid a bitter laugh: Maybe you really are from Uruguay.

I explained that I was not Uruguayan, that I had come for an academic conference, that this was my first time in the city. So you're a professor, said Adriano. The academy, said Fulvio, that's what we should have done, there you don't have to worry about epidemics, your living is safe. Just look at the Department of Social Praxis. I'd never heard of this department before. It's in the University, said Fulvio, there isn't anything like it anywhere, or at least that's what the ads said. Adriano wanted to know what I specialized in. I explained, and he asked if I'd seen the prison in Patricios, the Cárcel de Caseros. It's just a wall now, he said, they blew up the main buildings, and some artist did some stupid thing there. Foreign artists always come here and bring their stupid ideas about art, said Adriano. And then there's Devoto, but that's boring, everyone knows about that, or maybe you don't? I did know both prisons, I said, but nothing is more important than local knowledge in observing prisons and the spiritual structures that surround them. You see, said Adriano, there's a man who knows his limitations. Academic types can be very high-handed here. The lackey was about to speak, but Adriano silenced him. Keep your mouth shut, he said, the professor doesn't want to hear your theories.

I told Adriano that I was always interested in theories, whoever might propose them. He sighed and shook his head. They are of no consequence, Professor, Adriano said, they'll just muddy the waters—you saw it all last night, so you understand, don't you? I told him I did not understand him. The lackey went back to spraying the lilies and freesias, his spade-like shoulder blades working under his thin-looking skin. I know you just arrived, said Fulvio, but you really don't know? He took me by the arm (the avuncularity of this impeccable world) and escorted me back into the sunlight. Beyond the iron gate, now open, the green lawns rose and fell. Fulvio pointed out over them and said: You see any dogs there? He was right. No dogs, not one. I asked again where they went. He shook his head. If we knew that, he said, do you think we'd be suffering the way we are? They come out at night, they eat the meat, they drink the water, they come back, and then poof, nothing. A mower hummed. Strong and reverential. I wanted to tell Fulvio he had to be mistaken, but given the total absence of dogs—and I had seen hundreds, perhaps even thousands, fighting their way through that gap in the wall on Warnes—I couldn't. I suggested, instead, that he hire masons to brick up the hole, or fill it with rocks or wood himself, and he laughed in the same bitter, avian way his brother had. We tried that, he said, we tried that eight or nine times, maybe ten, and every time it was the same. The dogs came out after sundown anyway and when we ran to check the hole, our barricade was gone as if it had never been there in the first place. He blew on his fingertips. A small cloud of pollen leaped off them. Adriano said: It was like a magician came in and waved his wand.

All this meant that people no longer came to visit their relatives in the cemetery, Fulvio told me. I asked why, and he said I had to be kidding him. Don't they know in America what's going on down here? It's the dead, they come out at night in the form of dogs and visit their relatives. So why would anyone come in here anymore, when your relatives come right to your door? All those people died in the epidemic, Adriano said, and the dogs started showing up almost a year to the day after their burials. It's not just people who died in the epidemic, said Fulvio, because there was never any illness in Coronel Pringles and there are night dogs there now too. The teenage lackey nodded as his two masters spoke; he was, I guessed, Fulvio's son, he shared his broad brow and deep, impenetrably black nostrils. I had not heard the news of a recent epidemic afflicting Buenos Aires, but then again, I never paid attention to world affairs. So the epidemic I was prepared to accept, but Fulvio's theory of the night dogs I regarded as suspect, and I told him so. That's what everyone who isn't from around here says, he answered, you just wait till it happens in your city. My friend in Coronel Pringles thought I was full of shit too, and now he's pissing himself because the dogs have showed up there and he thinks he's going to go out of business. He runs a funeral parlor, replied Adriano, no way he ever goes out of business.

I took another step toward the cemetery lawn. If you don't believe me, said Fulvio, you can go check for yourself. I assured him that I did believe him, but he was already furious. You don't even know anything about this city, you've been here one night and you already think you're an expert, he shouted. His voice racketed through the marble entrance plaza, through the gates. My initial instinct, to flee, faded. I saw no reason why I should allow this flower salesman to bully me. As an expert on prison architecture, I was, by extension, an expert on the human body (a primordial prison) and the soul (the prisoner or alleged prisoner). I told him to calm down, I hadn't meant anything by it. It was a strange story, he had to admit. It's only strange, said Fulvio, if you want it to be strange. People think that because we landed on the moon, stuff like this doesn't happen anymore. Well, first of all, it was you people who landed on the moon, we never did, and second of all, that's a logical fallacy. The lackey came up behind Fulvio, eyes wide in fear. Adriano told his brother to calm down. I offered my hand to Fulvio. This gesture surprised me. I did not under ordinary circumstances engage in social theatrics. I'm usually a peaceable man, he said as he shook my hand, but on this issue, I just can't stay quiet. His palm dry and soft. Crossed by a scar. His skin left a golden smear of pollen on mine.

5.

AHEAD OF ME, AFLOAT in the dimness, a stripe of raw-looking flesh. I did not mention the coincidence to the cabbie as he drove along Directorio, and I held my tongue as he reached Avenida San Juan. I was waiting for him to speak. He did not. His silence was absolute. This exerted pressure on me, on my so-called soul, as it would have on the "soul" of any fellow primate. I asked about the dogs, since I could not ask about his carbuncles, i.e., his identity. He remained sunk in his marmoreal silence.

The buildings, mackerel-gray, salmon-rose, or white, empty white, wavered, ready to take wing. A common effect of insomnia. At doorsteps and lobby entrances, human figures knelt to place meat and pour water into steel bowls; many took the meat from silver freezer bags, while others dumped it out of plastic grocery bags; the water came from hoses, buckets, and pitchers. At a stoplight, I saw one pitcher shaped like a rooster, water leaping from its beak. Neighbors greeted each other as they might during any outdoor chore. The houses without these offerings looked desolate, a desolation increased by a lonely, muted noise filling the cab. A distant murmur, punctuated by occasional bell-like tones. I thought it was an eccentric engine sound, until the driver took his earphones out as we arrived at the social sciences building. It was music. Drums and cymbals overlaid, with shrill flute notes interrupting: the song I had first heard in the airport, the song I'd heard again pouring from the clerk's radio in the all-night shop on the corner of Emilio Mitre and Hualfín. My driver said it was called "Dog Symphony." He didn't know who wrote it, he didn't know how long it had been popular. It was always popular, he said, I think.

I was due to meet Ana in a lecture hall on the first floor of the social sciences building on Alvear. From the outside it resembled a small suburban hospital. I knew the layout of the building as well as I knew the layout of the city streets, thanks to the ample conference brochure I'd received. The first floor contained the main lecture rooms; above it, on the second floor, what an Argentine would call the first floor, was the sociology department, above that archaeology, then anthropology, economics, media studies, gender studies, and indigenous studies. History, where Ana served, was found on the eighth floor. Yet of the students themselves I knew nothing. Maps can tell you nothing about student moronism, sadly, other than where you are likely to find it. But as I passed among these hurrying adolescents, I understood how apposite Ana's remark had been: they were no more than burgherly poltergeists. Heads, lips, scarves, eyes. All these filled the air. Glances slid fluidly and blankly over my face, over the walls and the high, dirty ceiling. They moved with studied, I thought, freneticism, evincing all the might of the young, exuding the pitiable, vermiform energy that characterizes youth, especially student youth. And they like my own students were divided, they too comprised two armies. That I noted at once. Half the students, male and female alike, wore nylon chokers with dog ID tags attached to them. The tags chimed softly as they walked. Tag wearers spoke only to tag wearers; those with naked necks spoke only to those with naked necks. The music the cabdriver had listened to with devotion trilled and buzzed. From headphones buried in student ears the noise leaked out. It poured, as well, from the open door of a men's restroom, along with an ammoniac stink. The janitor plunging his mop into the mottled zinc bucket had a small radio affixed to his cart.

In a niche near the door of the lecture room we were scheduled to present in, a marble man in a marble suit with a marble mustache stood watch. Next to him, a fat, bald woman was waiting with two friends, both dark haired. One tall, her face oblong, and one short, her face also oblong. They weren't wearing tags. All three muttered to each other in quiet, rapid bursts, as if exchanging strings of obscenities. They paid no attention to me. The fat woman was saying that she did not understand why the department got all the funds for renovation, while in indigenous studies they had to starve. Her shorter interlocutor said: You knew it was going to go this way, you had to—that's why things have come to a head. Her taller interlocutor said that she didn't even consider the department real scholars. You lack a feeling for class consciousness, said the fat woman. I peered through the doorway into the lecture hall. I saw slumberous students, dust motes wheeling in a shaft of southern sunlight, and the low dais from which I would be delivering my talk. The table on the dais, around which the tiered seating rose up like ship walls, held two places, two notebooks, two pens, two blue folders. But no Ana.

I contemplated rushing to her office and rushing back. But I knew that if I left the exiguous audience would leave as well. There were no more than a dozen attendees. The fat, bald woman. The two women who had come in with her (they sat near the front, already taking notes; their pens made coleopteran scratching sounds). A boy with a blank, white face and well-greased hair. He belonged to the faction that wore dog ID tags. He was handsome; he looked, in fact, like a beardless Che Guevara. The students sat, silent or (in the case of the fat woman and her friends) whispering to each other. They avoided looking at me and I avoided looking at them. Instead, they looked through the tall windows that let out onto the quadrangle, and I looked as well. A woman passed by, wearing the sky-blue livery of the officers I'd seen at the airport. Then two men. Then another man, alone. The students seemed uneasy. One of them, I did not see who, whispered: I don't understand, I don't understand. His voice threatened to swell into a complaint, a howl, so I simply started talking, introducing myself and making excuses for Ana, and then launching into my presentation.

The two dark-haired women wrote down almost every word I said, at a speed I found incredible and mildly nauseating. I laid out my theories about the construction of the Butyrka. My hands sawed the air, to show the mighty sawing and chopping committed in the name of its architect, the Catherinite Matvey Kazakov. (In his absurd periwig.) Basement beneath basement, stone piled on stone. And all in full view of the city center. The Butyrka, of course, survived into the Soviet era, I said, and came into its own during the Great Terror, another thunderous and in-plain-sight occurrence. Therein—and this was the argument I had been refining—lay the true innovation of the Butyrka. Its endless adaptability, its capacious swallowing technique, identical for prisoners under the tsars and those taken by the commissars. As I made this remark, which had seemed especially moronic to me during my attempts to revise the paper, the two copyists at the front stood up and announced that they had a joint question: how could I, in good conscience, come and lecture them about the theory of prison architecture even as a new prison was being built before our very eyes? They spoke together, pens in hand, one voice alto and one soprano. Before I had even lifted my lethargic tongue from the floor of my mouth, the rest of the students in the audience began to jeer and whistle behind the copyists, or simply groan in anticipation. One called out: Don't answer, Professor, they always do this. It was the boy who looked like Che.

The women said nothing further, their mouths hard and eyes slightly glassy. In other words the expression induced by "radical discourse." I know student concerns. I won't say I understand them because there is, of course, nothing to understand. Student concerns and miseries amount to nothing, but if you tell a student this he will regard it as a victory, as proof you cannot comprehend his moral greatness. The correct way to defeat students is to hear them out while wearing a grave and serious expression, to let them tire themselves, exhaust themselves and their arsenal, and then simply ignore them. You don't even need to use the tools of authority. Beatings or tear gas, imprisonment, torture, and execution: all these only add strength to student moronism. I lowered my voice and asked them what their concern was, and the taller woman said that I must have noticed the meat bowls, no? And what did I think those were for? The first bricks in a new, metaphorical prison. The other students were really jeering now, shouting, swearing. The boy who had initially told me not to answer was calling them cunts, useless cunts.

The women started shouting a slogan: First ethics, then meat, first ethics, then meat. The other students had unplugged their headphones and the Dog Symphony—playing through six or seven tin-voiced speakers—competed with and almost obscured the four words. The boy who had called the slogan-shouters useless cunts stood up and threaded his way down the tiered floor between the desks, jerking his pelvis with Apollonian precision. The other students leaned or twisted their torsos to make room for his passage; his approach to the shouting copyists brought forth various hoarse cries of approval. The two shouters saw him approaching, but they just raised their voices and went on shouting as the whistles and yells from the spectating students grew denser, more harmonized, afloat, aloft. The boy who looked like Che had almost reached the shouters; both were eyeing him now with evident fear on their pale, lightly equine faces (I wondered if they were sisters) even as they raised their voices more and more and started to wave their soft-looking fists in the air (a diamond engagement ring caught the sunlight on one). Under ordinary circumstances I would simply have shouted for someone to go get security, but now, as these porteños displayed their youth, their student youth, I stepped off the dais, I rushed to interpose myself between the shouters and the boy. He saw me and told me to stay the fuck out of his way, and I saw that though he was much shorter than I am he was also much broader and better built. I ignored him and continued my advance. Stay back, Professor, this doesn't concern you, he said. The women went on shouting even after I had inserted myself between them and the boy. Get out of my way, he whined, get out of my way. I told him I would call campus security if he didn't leave, at once. Every student in attendance burst into harsh laughter as I said this. Even the shouters, who interrupted their chanting to laugh.

The boy shoved me. I did not abandon my position. I'm warning you, Professor, he said, I'm warning you one last time. I shrugged and crossed my arms, like a fool. He struck me with such speed that I never saw the blow coming. White light poured into my right eye. I stumbled over a bolted-down desk and smashed my head into the slick, dark wooden floor. First ethics, then meat, first ethics, then meat: the shouters kept up their chant through the boy's assault on me. Shut the fuck up, he said. The taller shouter answered: No way, and especially not for you, you dickhead. Her shorter friend went on shouting. Her voice was starting to fray. I'm not going to warn you again, said the boy, you saw what I just did to the professor, so you know I'm serious. This time it was the shorter woman who stopped shouting. To spit in his face. I had regained my feet now but the boy's blow had stunned me. An edema was already inflating where his fist had landed. The blow the floor struck, however, made my legs tremble, and so I could not reach the boy and the shouters in time, or so it seems to me from the standpoint of "historical memory." The boy stared at the shouters and they stared back, went on shouting, louder and louder, their larynges vibrating. Violent applause filled the air (from tag wearers only) as the boy struck the shorter woman in the mouth.

I managed to force myself forward, one step, one more. Like a crawling dog, I thought. My arm extended and my hand palpating nothing, the shouter's lips tearing, her bloody spittle starting to leak and spurt, along with the pearly human darkness behind her teeth, gaze, skin, hair, adipose tissue, the darkness lining her cunt and filling the balls of her assailant, carried by their joint bloodstream, lubricating their viscera and their brains, extending to the attic darkness above and the cellar darkness below, below the quadrangle grass, walled up in the libraries and dormitories, flooding the Paraná estuary and flooding the South Atlantic, brought to fruit among the subatomic processes of the sun. Phenomena, friends: they're wearing me out.

6.

THE MARBLE WALLS OF the bathroom beside the lecture hall: they can only be called refulgent. The light bouncing off them made my head hurt, no matter how often I lifted handfuls of water up to splash them on my face. And no matter how often I lapped at the faucet stream, the taste of blood still filled my mouth and throat.

Order had restored itself in the lecture hall when I returned. A chevron of blood marked the site where the boy who looked like Che had struck the shouter. She and her fellow morons had left behind leaflets piled neatly on their chairs. *First ethics, then meat.* The words from their chant. The remaining students could tell me only that security officers had taken Alma and the other girl, and Victor (the boy who looked like Che). I asked them if they knew Dr. Mariategui, the history professor; they all looked at me with wet pity in their eyes but gave no real answer. Is she a friend of yours, the short, obese young woman with the shaved-bald scalp asked me. I told her that we worked together, we were not friends. Well, said the bald woman, you should try to find her. Try to have her sort things out here for you. It's not good for foreigners to get involved with the University police, Professor. Even tangentially, like you did. This sentiment provoked opposition among the other attendees: No, that's not fair, they're just doing their jobs.

Outside the lecture hall, I found a fainter patch of blood shaped like a clover. From that a brief trail extended along the hallway, ending abruptly at the niche where the white marble statue and its white marble mustache awaited me with frightening equanimity. Two students were sitting and reading—one *A Universal History of Infamy* and the other *Hopscotch*—on a bench across from the statue; neither had seen the security officers, Alma, the other girl, or Victor, though they claimed, with a collusive snigger, to have been reading for at least an hour, if not longer. I pointed out the blood, viscid and bright. The Borges reader said simply: Fucking disgusting, but it's not my responsibility. The Cortázar reader didn't even answer. She let the author's too-wide-apart eyes, like those of a mantis, stare at me from the back cover.

All writers, the really talented ones at least, have stupid-looking eyes, I thought as I waited for the elevator in the central lobby. The student flow had dwindled to nothing. Only the apocrine scent of youth persisted. And from somewhere, possibly the radio affixed to the janitorial cart, the faint strains of the Dog Symphony. I had to find Ana. I hoped she would be able to explain this disturbance. It could not be the first or last of its kind, I knew, because the chain of student moronism stretches through all times and places. The chants of the women and the fury of the young man—these truly baffled me. The territory they imagined themselves to be contesting, that's what I hoped Ana could delineate. She would be at the cocktail reception the brochure had gone into surprising detail about, even listing the wines (all from Mendoza) that would be served. She had warned me about this reception in her last letter, saying that it was to be held on the departmental rooftop, in the rooftop garden. She had spoken of this rooftop garden with distaste and spleen, calling it an abode, a hutment, a bivouac, and other such terms. I was, despite my unease and my increasing headache, curious to see the object of her scorn and hopeful that she would at last be present.

Bloody flecks kept appearing on the white elevator floor. I looked directly at them and they vanished, an ocular trick played either by my injury or by my exhaustion. I whistled the same four note phrase over and over: a bar from the Dog Symphony. The elevator doors showed me a twisted, dulled reflection of my face (like an anti-Semitic caricature, with thick lips pursed around a button of void). The doors opened and I stepped forward. I almost injured myself again. The car was stopped short. At my waist, the grooved metal lip of the "floor." Above it, the cold, silent hallway leading to the offices of the history department. This hallway was floored in puce linoleum, scored with whitish scars. Beneath it, the grimy metal wall of the elevator shaft. A graffito, just under the lip, had been recently painted out. The elevator cab telephone normally used in such situations had been decapitated: frayed copper wires extended from the sawed-open brass tube.

I climbed out. The puce tiling as cold against my palms as the air. I pressed my aching orbit against it as I climbed out. When I had regained my footing I checked to make sure this infantile moment of mine had gone unobserved. Ana's name was not listed in the directory posted across from the elevators. I didn't know why this would be the case, and the most fantastic—also the most dull and domestic—justifications spun themselves out. That she had been fired and been too ashamed to tell me. That she had never worked at the University of Buenos Aires at all, that she was merely an academic impostor. That I myself had dreamed her up from the beginning. But she had

40

tenure (she'd written me the day she received it, saying that the water was now up to her eyebrows), which meant she still had her job. As for her existence and academic credentials, I'd read both her books, both published by the University of Buenos Aires Press. Unless those books were hallucinations, Pasternak, I murmured, this is merely an oversight.

The puce reception desk was empty. A puce fan sliced the air above the desk and the puce vinyl-clad chairs for visitors, standing in obscenely sad array on the puce carpet. The air here stank, not of sweat but of disinfectant, powerful esters, the stink of long-rotten bananas. I tried simply shouting: Hello? Only a damp echo met me. The history department, as I walked along its corridors, seemed to be in a state of physical tumult. Like that which precedes a move or follows a suicide. Open cardboard boxes standing outside doors, crammed with books and papers, photographs, eyeglasses, spare shoes, ossified knickknacks. The contents were all more or less identical from box to box. Almost all the doors stood open. Each had the name of its occupant painted on the ribbed, clouded glass panel in the upper half of the door, as if chiropractors were renting the rooms. The offices themselves looked scoured: the windows (transparent) and furniture (puce) stripped of human greasiness and its slavish ironies. Fingerprints, other oily affairs. Blank, broad planks of sheetrock were stacked against walls and in corners, on the upper and lower levels of the six double-decker contractor's trolleys I counted. The names on the doors obeyed no schema at all. I had to check each one individually to find Ana's. The department had two identical wings, precise images of each other, extending east and west from the elevator bank. In fact, Pasternak, I thought as I traversed them, they might as well be mirrors reflecting each other, and you might as well be passing from mirror to mirror. An inane thought. I could not rid myself of it. The cold stagnant air seemed itself to conceal a deep snigger. My shoes squeaked abominably. On my second pass, between *De Gandia* and *Zinny*, I found Ana's door: *Mariategui*, in the black and gold pseudomedical font the historians had chosen to record their own names.

The door itself was closed. A dark, vague shape was visible through the glass—but I could not determine who or what it was, so I knocked. No answer. I tried the handle: locked stiffly in place. I tried again, pressing myself timidly against the wood of the door, as though my added weight might somehow spring the lock. A shuffling, vague murmur came from within the office. I called out: Hello? Ana? It's me. Are you there? The same nausea that had assailed me as I attempted to work in the Pensión Vermesser assailed me once more now. I kept trying, repeating myself, knocking and jiggling the handle, but the silence within was now absolute. If this is a joke, I said, it's not funny—Ana, this sort of humor is beneath you, and if it's not you in there, come out anyway. That final absurdity echoed through the empty hall, but elicited no response. Or only a notional one. I thought I heard a deep chuckle within my friend's office. Not her own. Her laugh was short, precise, and dry; this was damp and sloppily comprehensive. It didn't happen again. I pressed my ear against the warming glass and noted the greasy stain my skin left. I heard nothing. Another dream, another fantasy, like the bloodstains on the elevator floor.

This area is off-limits to the public, sir, a rich, calm voice said. A woman in sky-blue livery was striding down the corridor. Her cap could not contain the lustrous mass of her dark hair. Next to her upper lip, a dense-looking, circular mole. I explained that I was not a member of the public, that I was here to look for my colleague, and that I had come at the invitation of the University, of Ana Mariategui and Professor Sanchis Mira. The officer's silver nameplate read LUXEMBURG. Around her tall, slender throat a silver whistle hung from a leather cord, and attached to this cord was one of the golden, rabbit-shaped labels I'd seen earlier. I've never heard of the Pampas hare, I told the officer. It's a well-known animal, she said, there's a real infestation of them in certain areas. Whoever found out you could make leather from them is a benefactor to humanity. The chuckling sound came again from Ana's office. I leaned against the door, pressed my ear to the glass. Nothing more. Dr. Mariategui went home, said Luxemburg. It's been a tiring time for the people who work here, as you can see. They're just getting ready to remodel. What is your name, sir? I told her. She did not say: Like the guy who wrote *Doctor Zhivago*. This is how I was usually greeted when I revealed my name. Instead, she asked for identification. I handed her my driver's license. She chewed her lip (red, wet-looking) as she peered at it, peered into the digestive pupil of the state. I'm afraid that I can't accept this. There's been a municipal ordinance about documentation. Do you have your passport?

A pistol shone in a holster on her hip. The history of armaments prison guards carried was by necessity a small part of my study. This was, I saw, a Browning, a nine-millimeter, known among my colleagues as *dvuglavvy orel*, a double eagle. Both military and civilian security forces employed it. Ana was the first to explain the history of this term, which stretched back to the second decade of the fifteenth century. Then, it referred to the two-billed halberds favored by the guards of the Piombi in Venice. The ventilation muttered, and again the wet, baritone chuckle sounded within Ana's office. Officer, I just want to see if everything is alright, I said. The panic I had expected to constrict my throat, to bring sweat to my forehead and palms failed to inflame me. Due to my injuries, or to the frank impossibility of my regarding this security officer as a "real" policewoman. She was as much a burgherly poltergeist as the students, Pasternak, a ghost. That's how I explained my refusal internally. If you don't have your passport, sir, I'm afraid I need you to leave, said Luxemburg, in her viscous, anechoic voice, as if I had not spoken. I can escort you to the reception for visiting scholars, or I can escort you off the premises, it's your choice, Mr. Pasternak. I tried the handle of Ana's office again. Sir, please come with me, she said. I understand you're upset, but you should speak to the boss about your friend. Her hard fingers pressed into my biceps. Their heat perceptible. Sickly light smeared on her cap bill, her holster, her belt, the black butt of her baton. And her boots, patent leather, in which my own attenuated and already half-forgotten form was reflected.

7.

THE SUN HAD SUNK below the toothed skyline of Recoleta. Its last rich tints colored the air orange, lilac, and crematory gray. The roof garden was already crowded, and the crowd was already rendered indistinct by approaching night. The garden deserved all the scorn Ana had poured on it. It could only be considered a garden because of the pergola edging the roof, which was made of odorous unweathered pine. From it dangled Christmas lights in uneven loops and sky-blue streamers.

Cindery tiles and patches of naked tar formed the "earth" here. At the center of the garden a long trestle table covered in a white cloth held two steel bowls, like the meat and water bowls before Violeta's door, before the University's, before all doors I had seen. Nothing filled them. In the northwest corner, a white metal shed emitted the sweet smell and clotted sound of frying. Waiters wearing white shirts and black pants dashed out of this shed, carrying bottles of red wine on silver trays, pouring drinks for the partygoers. Luxemburg had left me alone by the door of the emergency staircase. Guests appeared to be using this because of the elevator problem. She had joined the other officers patrolling the roof edge, staring down at the quadrangles to the east and south. She clearly enjoyed command over this squad. She moved from officer to officer, patting their shoulders or talking to them, joking around, offering them cigarettes from a sky-blue case. I expected her to keep harassing or threatening me once we reached the rooftop, but as soon as we stepped out and the cinders rustled under our soles, she stopped paying any attention to me.

I had come to find Sanchis Mira. Ana's absence worried me. Her locked office door and the gulping noise I'd heard within worried me, though again I dismissed these worries as sentimental. Sanchis Mira would be able to reassure me, but I knew nothing about him: his first name, what he looked like, his height or weight. I knew that his last name was shared by a company that manufactured turrón, a disgusting nougat candy that Ana and I discovered in Córdoba. And I remembered Ana's statement that he had once been a professor of French. But that would not help me locate him in the crowd on the roof, all former or present professors of French (professors of coprophagia beneath the chandeliers, in Ana's phrase) in spirit if not in fact. I could not walk from partygoer to partygoer and ask if they happened to know where Sanchis Mira was. Rather, I could have, but it would have required engaging in fast, trivial conversations, a skill I never mastered. Instead I waited and stared at each male face as it passed. Was he this obese man with the face of a disappointed pederast, like an inflated latex mask? Was he the cadaver swaying in the night breeze as he stared down into the quadrangles? I did not know, and because I did not know, every middle-aged man became him, impersonated him, consumed and excreted him, I thought, yet not one was him, not one could touch the essential being. I realized I was mouthing these absurd sentiments as I stared, which explained the visual hostility that met me, and also explained the cyclonic pattern the waiters formed as they whirled across the roof carrying their trays and their black bottles, ignoring me. It explained the migraine blossoming, along with flashes of ocular white, within my skull, and the fact that whenever I closed my eyes against the pain I saw again the blinding marble benches outside La Chacarita.

The wines of Mendoza have no equal anywhere in the world, said a strong, warm voice. I opened my eyes. This voice emanated from beneath a roach-colored mustache echoing the hard horizon. On it, smears of final chalky light. You are Dr. Pasternak, said the bearer of this mustache, this earthly-law mustache. Yes, I replied. Captain Luxemburg pointed you out. I'm Sanchis Mira, and we should have been introduced before. He explained that he was the new head of the Department of Social Praxis. The Department had absorbed administrative responsibility for the prison studies conference, he added. He apologized again for the misunderstandings that had plagued, as he put it, my time in his bailiwick so far: the interruption of my lecture, the lack of any organized reception. His warm voice easily overcame the shouts drifting up from the campus. Someone was trying, near the walls of the building beneath us, to start up a cry of *First ethics, then meat.* His small, reddened eyes quivered as he noted the auscultatory stance which I'd assumed without meaning to. A waiter came up and proffered glasses of wine. My host, my chief host, went on: As a professor you will learn to ignore the brutal sentimentality of students, he said (though I was already a professor). The current climate on the fields (his phrase) of the social sciences faculty was not safe for a foreign academic. The student agitators who interrupted you (he meant the women) were well known to the University security services, as was the boy who criminally assaulted them. True, he said, only the boy had technically committed a crime, the propagation of false historical ideas violated no law, but the agitators were guilty as well, though that, he knew, must be hard for an outsider to understand.

The cry grew and grew in strength. More throats offered themselves up to it. Guards in sky blue leaned over the parapet to observe the shouting students. I asked Sanchis Mira if he knew how I could get in touch with Dr. Mariategui. I am unfamiliar with that name, sir, Sanchis Mira said. His eyebrows (much thinner and frailer-looking than his mustache, with widely spaced individual hairs visible) bent into a fatherly frown. I gave Ana's particulars: a historian, in my field, about my age, dark haired. I left out certain other particulars, namely Gogol and Pascal, and I said nothing about my attempted incursion. Sanchis Mira arranged the flukes of his mustache. The guards, I saw, had drawn their guns and were aiming them into the quadrangle, where the cries were most voluminous, most pure. Not from here you couldn't, Luxemburg shouted, it's too far. You must know her, I said. I do not, I am afraid, said Sanchis Mira. I am an administrator now and I do not meddle in the affairs of scholars. I was a scholar myself once, sir, a professor of French, and I remember how offensive the interference of administrators was to me. All the administrative work heading the new department required is distasteful to me, but I nonetheless have to perform it. Social praxis, Mr. Pasternak, he said, social praxis and its mysteries.

Hecklers had now begun to catcall and hurl obscenities at the "ethics-firsters." Shut up, shut the fuck up, a hoarse female voice shouted again and again. Luxemburg cackled each time. She was now looking down the barrel of her pistol into the quadrangle. Impossible. I attempted to move past Sanchis Mira, but the crowd was too dense. My headache had worsened. The white blooms of pain patchily obliterated the gathering darkness. Not from here, it's impossible, Luxemburg cried again. Through the white shed's doorway a new squad of waiters darted, each carrying a steel platter piled with dark slabs. Roast meat. A waiter proffered a platter. The smell nauseated me. Nonetheless, saliva leaped into my mouth. Sanchis Mira took a slab of meat from the platter and held it up for examination. He brought it close to his nose and inhaled. He noted my failure to take up a slab, and—with the meat near his nostrils—said, Mr. Pasternak, surely you won't refuse our meager hospitality? If I refused, it would mean an end to the conversation, which would mean an effective end to my search for Ana. Nausea, another wave of it, made my stomach flutter. Mr. Pasternak, please, said Sanchis Mira. He himself took another slab and offered it to me. The waiter forced his way through the crowd. Hands emerged, so to speak, from the darkness and removed slab after slab from his platter, and thick cries of delight surrounded his progress. I had no choice, now. I accepted the meat. Its scent, blunt and mildly cloying, almost made me vomit. But its overwhelming (historiographic) flavor, which I could not identify, calmed my nausea instantly, and the liquefied fat leaking onto my tongue silenced my so-called "inner voice." Sanchis Mira held his wineglass in one hand and his meat in the other, tearing it repeatedly with his enormous, tile-like, incandescent teeth.

As we ate, a crowd built up around the long white table, forming two writhing lines. There, on the roof, the guards abandoned their posts to help shepherd these lines and to answer the questions from the partygoers waiting in them. Soon, soon, said Luxemburg. The words slipped through the gap in the systolic/diastolic cries now rising more loudly, more shrilly, from the quadrangles, where the ethics-firsters and their opponents spurred each other to greater and greater heights of student moronism. The evening's entertainment, said my host. He clasped my biceps, as Luxemburg had done, and the grease on his fingers stained my suit jacket. To remove myself from his grasp would have been an even greater insult than refusing the meat, so I accompanied him, as I had accompanied Luxemburg, through the crowd—it parted around him, turning up its arrayed, moist eyes in respect—to the table set with the white cloth and steel bowls, now illuminated by a cone of baronial glare from a tall aluminum-bodied lamp. Money filled the steel bowls. Bills and coins, pesos, dollars, euros, rubles, yen, Turkish lira, even Kenyan shillings, which I recognized only because I had written a paper in graduate school about the *chastnyye polyany* (a term in my field designating the places in a prison used by the staff and guards, not by prisoners, i.e., the barracks, the offices, the private kitchen and eating rooms) of the Kamiti in Nairobi.

Two guards in sky blue, their hands on their pistols, flanked the table and stared straight ahead. The crowd around me thrust their arms out and handed money to a waiter behind the table, who counted it, noting the amounts and names, and asked: Left or right? This waiter bore the marks of a severe beating, two greenish edemas around his right eye, jammy blood in the cut on his torn lips, a blue bruise on his cheek, his left ear swollen. Hello, sir, he said to Sanchis Mira, will you be playing tonight? A wet, ragged sound came from his chest as he breathed. Sanchis Mira removed his wallet—an enormous wallet made of red leather. It too bore the golden label GENUINE PAMPAS HARE. The injured waiter would not look at me or at anyone else. He kept his eyes on Sanchis Mira as he took my host's money. I thrust a sheaf of dollars at him, to see if he would at last look up. He did not, though he did speak to me: Left or right, he asked. I hesitated. Sanchis Mira said: It's a simple question, Mr. Pasternak. Now is no time to play Hamlet in Russia. I said left; my money went into the left bowl. Academic bodies behind me emitted academic warmth. A loud whistle interrupted this churning. All the partygoers clustered around the bowl table stopped moving and the bruised waiter slammed an oblong Lucite cover over the two bowls. Ladies and gentlemen, ladies and gentlemen, Sanchis Mira was repeating.

He had at last released my bicep. The crowd was surging to the edge of the roof, pulling me along, among the wet eyes, wet mouths, wet hearts, and wet assholes. The guards stayed behind with the money. The waiter stared off into the vacant night. I almost stumbled among the rushing spectators, but I righted myself—stumbling now would have constituted an irremediable defeat. From the grit-covered parapet, the vista looked simple, even meager. On the other side of the University buildings, into the newspaper-colored distance, a long, irregular banner of waste ground stretched. It was lit by floodlights mounted on steel poles. I could not determine its borders, and the sickening notion apparated or even coalesced: it reached to the sea, Pasternak, to the Atlantic. The floodlights aided this illusion. They were too widely spaced, making it harder to observe the field. In their closed circles of glare you saw every grass-blade, every gleaming, water-filled depression. As a result, in the darkness beyond the glare almost nothing could be seen. Silence?

No. A guest, his features obscure in the dimness, leaned next to me, breathing hard. The tarry scent of wine poured out with every exhalation. Factitious ticking. Sanchis Mira was holding up a dim silver pocket watch. Other than that you could say it was quiet.

The waste field spread before us under the chaotic and useless floodlights, a simple and unreal cloth. I asked this dim guest what we were supposed to be watching, and he hissed: Shut the fuck up, you have to be quiet, otherwise it could be considered undue intervention. As he finished his sentence, a dog trotted up to a light pole and lifted its leg. The white brilliance washed out the dog's rufous fur to a brick-pink; its shadow trembled on the grass and my heart trembled as well. The animal was a bull terrier. It carried itself with humble strength. Its collar blinked, as it slowly circled the pole, like an eye, like a blinded eye. Like a heliograph, Pasternak, or a heliotrope blossom, I thought. Another dog ambled through the light, this one gun-colored, hugely tall, and bulky-chested. A mastiff. The two nosed each other's anuses. Their grumblings reached the spectators on the roof, who maintained their silence. Sanchis Mira's pocket watch was still aloft. Now more dogs arrived, trooping out of the darkness with easy serenity. Dog by dog, a pack of thirteen formed. The reddish dog, the mastiff, a spotted spaniel, two German shepherds standing side by side, an obese puli the color of crematory smoke, a dock-tailed pit bull, a borzoi whose fawn fur had been shaved almost to the skin, a Saint Bernard asleep next to the light pole, a bloodhound resembling (as all bloodhounds do) a prelate or dictator, and three mutts, grayish-brown, who crouched flank to flank in the half dark edging the floodlight pool.

The man standing next to me was getting excited. His breathing grew deep and coarse. His saliva itself, I suspected, took on a rustic smell. The odor of cooked meat, cooked fat, lymph, blood, the odor of civilization. Or is it culture? It spread, drifted, and lingered. The tick, tick, tick the pocket watch released into the night, like a naked human pulse—my own pulse slowed to match it, though that might simply be an aestheticized memory. Down on the waste field, a new shadow danced. A human shadow. A woman's. I could not make out her features at this distance. I saw she was a brunette, that's all. At rest on her shoulder a metal rail or joist. Sanchis Mira held a thick, short silver tube to his lips, connected to a leather cord that encircled his neck, and blew through it. Producing another silence, one inflated to near-bursting. The dogs raced toward the brunette on the field. She cried out. In defiance or despair.

8.

WHEN I RETURNED TO the Pensión Vermesser, Violeta was shaking meat from a silver bowl into a silver bag by the steps. The morning was overcast, the sky milk white. You keep student hours, Mr. Pasternak, said my hostess.

I sat on the chilly steps and observed her. I had not slept, not at all, and though my headache had dissipated, my eyelids abraded my eyes every time I blinked. I found myself forgetting, from moment to moment, the placement of my feet, my hands, my cigarettes. Images from the roof garden trembled in my memory. The ease with which the dark-haired woman had struck down the pack of dogs, one after the other. A truly philosophical demolition. I did not understand why the University was engaged in sponsoring such fights, even if only indirectly. And Violeta's "explanation" did not help. The clubs of Hecate, she said, that's what they call themselves. She'd never personally seen any that centered around betting on fights, but knew of gatherings that met regularly to bet on other night-dog activities—the speed with which a certain dog will reach La Chacarita, for example, or whether this or that meat bowl will be visited, or even which dog "belongs" to which human family, all these existed and were even well known; *La Nación* had recently published an article on them called, she thought, "Fortune's new friends."

And I hope, she went on—perhaps because I said nothing—that the dogs haven't lowered your opinion of the city. I always sleep through their appearance and in any case my immediate family is all alive, as far as I know. That's why I just refreeze and defrost the same steaks, she said, they never visit me anyway, and you have to save money where you can. Before I could ask the next logical question, i.e., why she put out bowls at all if the dogs never came to the Pensión Vermesser, she was already smiling and speaking: And you know very well, Mr. Pasternak, that as a hotelkeeper I have to go along with tradition, even if I am skeptical of it. Otherwise my business would suffer.

My need to speak with Ana, to confirm her involvement in all this, had deepened during my long walk home. The jubilant screams from the small segment of the crowd that bet on the woman and the disgusted sighs from those who had bet on the dogs—these I recalled with perfect clarity. I did not object to the killing of the dogs. The only alternative was for the woman to have been torn apart by their teeth, as if by a storm. The scene had nonetheless left me uneasy. Yet if Ana was involved with this, then I too could permit myself to remain involved. A sophomoric induction, Pasternak. I tried to find Ana's personal phone numbers, home and cellular, but I discovered that her entry in my address book contained only her phone number at the University. This increased my dizziness, and revived the floodlit nausea I had experienced on the rooftop. I remembered having written down her personal phone number sometime during our third year as friends, while she was reading Pascal in my bed, in a stiff wavering circle of lamplight. Or possibly Gogol. Yet now: nothing. As if in disproof of the esoteric theories I was beginning, automatically, to construct, my books lay open and naked on the desk, my spare shirts hung whitely in the closet, my socks and underwear cowered in the uppermost dresser drawer, and my razor stared from the migraine-yellow porcelain cup on the sink rim. All where I had left them, all as I had left them. Sleeping the trustful sleep of objects.

The phone book on the table listed four Mariateguis. One was Violeta's doctor friend; the two others also had male first names. The third was a woman, and though her first name, Jacinta, was not my colleague's first name, I tried anyway. I reached an answering machine, which played a long segment of the Dog Symphony before the message began. The woman it belonged to was clearly young. Her voice was an octave higher than my colleague's. I left nine or ten seconds of silence on her answering machine as retribution. The lilac stems in the vase next to the telephone, curved like two canine grins, mocked me. I could think of nothing else to do, so I called her number at the history department again, expecting either the goatish song of the busy signal or sheer nothing. To my shock, a male voice answered after the first ring: Department of Social Praxis. It was so similar to Sanchis Mira's that I slammed down the greasy, green receiver in fear. Sweat lined my armpits, my perineum, my forehead. The ashen taste of the Macedonias, a really putrid brand, lined my mouth. Violeta's song cut off and then resumed indoors. I lifted the phone and dialed yet again. The dry male voice announced once more: Department of Social Praxis. I asked for Dr. Ana Mariategui and the operator told me to wait. During the pause, I heard nothing, at first, and then a cheap and melancholy piano tune, which I recognized but couldn't identify. All music says the same thing, in the end. There's no need to specify what it is. Yet I struggled to recall the name of this melody and failed. The operator came back on and said that Dr. Mariategui was not available, but that he would be happy to pass on a message to her. I asked if I could come see Dr. Mariategui, what her office hours were. I added that I was a visiting academic she had sponsored, that I was attending a conference, but the operator interrupted me before I could explain about my field of research.

You need to come in to discuss such matters, sir, he said (I realized his voice was nothing like Sanchis Mira's, nothing at all) and began without preamble to read a list of dates and times. I missed the first three and asked him to repeat them. He answered: Do you want to resolve the issue or should I just report you to our administrators? The earliest time we have, in any case, is the day after tomorrow, is that soon enough? I told him no and apologized (for what crime I did not know). The operator said nothing. Hello, I said, hello? One moment, sir, said the operator, I want to make sure I am getting this down correctly. You are declining to come in for an interview. I assured him that there was no need for me to come in, I merely needed an address. Coming in for an interview is in my experience the best way to handle matters of this kind, sir, said the operator. His voice was clotted. As if with hidden laughter. I replied that I did not have the time at the moment, though I regretted this fact. It is regrettable, sir, said the operator, and asked me how to spell my last name. I did; I waited for him to ask if I was related to the famous Pasternak, the author of *Doctor Zhivago*. But he did not. He coughed, or grunted, or choked back another laugh, and said that he was now seeing an address entered in the record for Dr. Mariategui: Avenida Julio Zenz 4300. I thanked him. The saliva filling my mouth blurred the word; droplets spurted out onto the octagonal table, and a few, to my disgust, even hit the lilac. If you should decide to come in, sir, he went on, as I highly recommend, please remember to bring an ID and proof of travel. A plane ticket, anything like that. Otherwise we would have no idea whether you actually came to Buenos Aires.

The city atlas I'd brought with me (my memory for maps is tremendous but not infallible) did not depict Avenida Zenz. No mention in the index and none in the brief, dead biographies of famous sites the atlas offered as ancillary entertainment. I peered and peered through a magnifying glass framed in frail puce plastic and attached with a nylon cord to the book itself, but I saw no Zenz; in the lowest desk drawer I found a telephone directory and was leafing through it in the hopes of discovering a dweller on Zenz at random—a desperate, frivolous hope, I admit—when Violeta called to me from the parlor threshold. She was flushed from the housecleaning. She carried a blue-and-white checked rag and a plastic spray bottle full of pinkish liquid (like blood and rendered fat, mingling). Sweat beads decorated her hairline, and through the loose armholes of her shirt I saw the dark tufts in her deep axillae flaring. She asked me if something was wrong. I assured her that no, everything was fine, that I was fine. She told me I looked exhausted, though my exhaustion had long since left me, it had drained away on my journey home, or during the rooftop events, or at another point in the ichorous flow. I explained my predicament. She knew exactly where Avenida Julio Zenz was. I was ashamed. After all, so far I had conducted my (external) affairs with perfect alacrity and poise, and the Zenz affair represented a defeat, that I could not deny. She said Zenz was a new street, or a new name for an old street in La Boca; it used to be Parker. The writer it was renamed to honor just died, she said, in the epidemic. There's no way they could have updated the maps. So don't blame yourself, Mr. Pasternak.

La Boca, The Mouth. Every tourist knows the name of that barrio, Pasternak. It's famous throughout the world. I ordinarily would never have visited such a place. On my travels I preferred to find the truly anonymous, truly empty zones of a city. I was never perfectly successful, and this trip had occasioned many hindrances. La Boca was home to the Boca Juniors, a soccer team. Soccer is another prison, in which the wardens and guards outnumber the inmates by a thousand or ten thousand to one. And while Caminito was crowded, and while the houses as I walked south displayed colors (red, orange, yellow, pink) corrupted by the endless viewing. This complexion did not last. The Riachuelo, dull and metallic, visually impure, flowed alongside me as I crossed Alfredo Palacios, a street named after an Argentine senator. The first socialist, if memory serves, in the Chamber of Deputies. A man with an imitative mustache meant to suggest some Russian exploder. His name repeated now by blue, silent plaques among sheds with corrugated aluminum sides that filled most of the street lots here, among the shrill metallic cries of saws or drill presses. The smell of the river poured lazily through the silent air between the sheds. I looked into the few stores that I passed. One sold only hubcaps, another orthotic shoes, the walls of a third glittered telegraphically with key blanks. The Dog Symphony trembled and trilled from a radio in the orthotic shoe store. All three, of course, had meat bowls set out. All six bowls were empty. The key-store owners had housed theirs under a wooden roof cut from a lemon crate (you could see the painted, ruined lemons) and shingled with oxidized keys.

I found Parker quite quickly, or Avenida Zenz, as it was now known. Its new nameplate was smaller than the old one, and a whitish penumbra surrounded it against the dirtied brick wall. The city had shown Zenz a great dishonor in naming this street after him. I didn't know the man's work, of course; I've never had time for contemporary literature. But even so: Parker (or Zenz) was one block long. This was why, I assumed, it had been chosen. So that minimal damage would be done to existent atlases. Atlases, census records, subway maps—all these the great city values more than a dead or dying writer. Notwithstanding the shit-flecked fan dances porteños perform if Borges or Cortázar enters the conversation. Zenz (or Parker) ran from Coronel Salvadores to California; I was standing at the California end, staring along the street into a barren triangular field on Salvadores. The little street was silent, sentried by one lone leafless poplar. The Riachuelo's hard glints fired whenever I looked east and south, beyond the thrumming sheds that separated Zenz from the concrete shingle and the water. Above me a vapid sky in which geese honked as they flapped.

I had trouble locating 4300. A building that occupied an entire city block filled the northeast side of Zenz corner to corner. The largest shed I'd yet seen. A monstrous building clad in curd-colored aluminum siding. It looked as I had always imagined the exterior of the Labyrinth to look, but buildings that recall the Labyrinth have become sadly common in all cities. Near its roofline, a blue scrawl of graffiti said: YOUR MOTHER FUCKS NIGHT DOGS. The hand neat and sure, like the hand of a copyist, an eighteenth-century expert flowing on and on through the constellations. I circumnavigated the building, all four sides, thinking it might be 4300. I saw no entry door, no windows, just the blank siding through which came a mild, mechanical hum. Eight bowls, two to a side. Nothing exceptional there. I rested my forehead against the metal—the absence of other pedestrians stripped me of shame—and the vibrations soothed me. My eyelids began to fall. But this strange building was obviously not 4300, so I had to abandon my soothing, subterranean phenomenon.

On Zenz's southwest side spread a low, dark structure: an octagonal one-story building with a hooked annex encircling its parking lot. This lay behind a massive, rusted fence. A row of blue vans gleamed in the lot, more or less like blue molars. Or the late-afternoon light itself might have possessed this dental quality. I don't know, our lives are governed to a certain extent by dental mysteries far more than religious mysteries. But in any case I crossed and surveyed. I was sure that this barracks-like structure would also fail to be what I wanted, that the departmental operator had played an easy, cruel prank on me, but as I approached I saw that the low building was indeed 4300 Zenz. The name spelled out in umber letters beneath the ragged awning was OJEA MEAT DISTRIBUTORS. I saw no sign of life within. The side windows were small and high up like portholes, filthy and covered with metal netting. An empty desk was visible through the dead window in the steel front door; a toy Argentine flag dangled stiffly from its black dowel planted in a pot clearly meant to hold silk flowers. I pressed the button next to this steel door. The buzzer shrilled within, but nothing else happened. The meat and water bowls left here seemed to be hammered from the same dead, crude metal as the door. The blue vans in the lot, parked obliquely, displayed the words MAN'S BEST FRIEND SOCIETY in a dizzying array. Orthodontic. Or heterodontic. My blood thudded at my temples. The silence of the street magnified this drumbeat. Another wedge of geese bumbled east above me. The sun and moon occupied the sky at the same time. The pitted fence abraded my fingers as I laced them through its links. All the preconditions for a "literary" occurrence manifested themselves, and a sick, viscous elation was curdling in my bowels.

The octagonal building had another door, also of grayish steel, set into its western arm. A door meant to give workers access, I imagined, to these dental, echoing vans. This door opened and a fat, hairy-shouldered man in a white undershirt stepped through, his boot treads creaking against the asphalt of the lot. As the door closed behind him I saw, or imagined I saw, sky-blue cloth, banners or uniforms. The fat man didn't see me at first. His cigarette lighter failed and he had to resort to matches. Clusters of brown, faint stains speckled his undershirt. Fresher red streaks painted his wide forearms. From the Ojea building, as from the metal sheds in its vicinity, metal whines and cries drifted, treble and sustained. The fat man paced without seeing me, slapped the flank of the lead van in fraternal affection, scratched his balls. In short, a fellow primate. I called out to him: Sir, sir. He ignored me. Or the noise from the Ojea building obscured my words. But eventually, after repeated calls, he stared at me, one hand on the truck side, his cigarette in the other, an image fit only to be smeared with the effluvium of artistic photography, in fact, especially because more geese had appeared and their crooked, tender shadows were touching the asphalt. I waited, I called out again, and the fat man approached without speaking. The blood drying on his skin carried a raw smell. He stared at me through the fence, stared without speaking when the name Mariategui made its appearance, stared and stared. I asked again: Sir, do you know Dr. Mariategui, Ana Mariategui? A colleague of yours? A supervisor? I was given this address by the Department of Social Praxis.

The fat man spat through the chain-link with astonishing precision. The sputum traveled over my shoulder but passed close enough to my face to cause me to leap back. Then he apologized, but a crooked and even ashamed grin twisted and crushed his apology. I did not mean to do that, spit so close, but I have to spit constantly, it's an affliction, said the fat man. He spat again. Who knows if it was genuine spit and a genuine affliction or a theatrical proof of his previous statement? I asked him if he knew anything, anything at all about Dr. Mariategui, I said once more I'd been given this address by the Department of Social Praxis. You work there, he wanted to know. I told him no. You don't look like it but I thought I'd ask, he went on. He spat a third time, between his own feet. I don't know that name, he said, and I don't know why the University sent you here. We're a meat packaging company, as I'm sure you figured out. He grinned his broken-spined grin once more, and I saw that fading bruises, faint and greenish, mottled his face and bare arms. Please, I said, I must know, so if you're fucking with me please stop. My own profanity surprised me.

I'm not fucking with you, sir. I honestly don't know anyone by that name, or anything about the Department of Social Praxis, beyond what I said already. He was smiling, his tile-like teeth strong and dark yellow, his gums vivid. Then why did they give me this address, I asked, it can't be a mistake—the street was just renamed. That's true, said the spitter, his smile twisting and curling into horns, knives, a trident. Whatever you like. Yes, he said, that has confused people. As he spoke his pupils twitched, and I followed their arc. They had twitched toward a gate in the parking lot fence, closed with a loosely wrapped chain. I wish I could help you, sir, said the spitter, through his pollen-colored smile, I wish I could but I don't know anything and only employees are authorized to be on the premises. Again his pupils jumped, again they indicated this gate in the fence, secured by its frivolous chain. A gate I could enter if I liked. And at the spitter's invitation, so to speak, I was already heading toward this door, my molars already locked behind my own painful and obedient grin. The spitter's smile had widened, as had the blank, titanically empty smile of the sky, the roofline, this deserted precinct. We had reached the gate, and I was waiting for the spitter to unwrap the chain when the door he had first exited opened again. A rat-faced boy in a sky-blue uniform with silver epaulettes leaned through and shouted: Olegario, get inside, what the fuck is the matter with you. The spitter looked at me. Real melancholy in his muddy eyes. He obeyed the uniformed boy. He glanced at me again before the door closed. One meager raindrop stroked my earlobe. Then another.

9.

THAT GUY IS A real motherfucker, Adriano muttered, or so
I hear. He was holding another match (whose flame I could
hardly see in the glaring sunlight) to the black mouth of his
pipe.

He meant Sanchis Mira. I told him everything about my bizarre evening on the roof while we were waiting in line at the
Cárcel de Devoto. He listened with grave care, nodding, squint-
ing, tapping more brick-brown tobacco into the bowl. He added
that while he wished he'd been a professor he was glad he didn't
have to deal with them. He pointed at the squadron of University police standing guard around the entrance gates (next to
the two steel bowls reflecting sunlight). Adriano turned out to
know even more about the phenomenon of betting on dogs than
Violeta did. The clubs of Hecate, he said, that's nothing new. We
had those under Videla and we had them under Rosas, too, it's
just part of our history. Not always dogs, though—at least that's
what it said in the article. And he wasn't surprised, he added,
about my friend. It happens all the time, he said, it started right
after the epidemic too. Even before the night dogs showed up.

The line was composed mostly of old women wearing black
kerchiefs striped with lilac. The liveried guards let them in five
or six at a time, not bothering them or berating them. They

asked for identification and then proffered their upturned caps. The first time I watched an old woman drop coins (they chittered telegraphically) into the cap, I found the gesture so nonsensical that it failed to make any impression, sordid or comical, at all. Adriano already held a fistful of change ready, taken from his wallet which, like the fobs his brother sold, also bore a GENUINE PAMPAS HARE label. I gathered up all the centavos (with their bloody smell) I had in my pockets. The cap the guard at the line's head offered me displayed a sweat stain on the inner crown, shaped like a pretentious, second-rate nation.

The layout of the carcel did not correspond in any way to the plans of it I had seen. The prison had long been a basic instructional text for aspirants to my field. We all knew it by heart. Even my colleagues whose memories fell short of mine at least knew the carcel. When the structural changes had been made, Adriano didn't know exactly. Some time after the epidemic, he said. The oblong garrison you passed through to enter was still there but in the center of the courtyard the fences I remembered from my studies had been demolished, creating a wide, broken-skinned expanse of concrete across which the old women moved with complete freedom, their striped kerchiefs fluttering. From the cracks in the asphalt grew rugged dandelions. The old ladies gathered up handfuls of these as they passed, crammed them into their purses or carried them tenderly in curled hands.

The tiered cellblocks—once the residences of luminaries, of the southern capital's most phosphorescent luminaries—had been torn down. Their foundations remained, jagged, periodontal, enclosing patches of gravel, gray stones into which lines of blue stones had been set. On the last remaining walls, the outer walls, black oblong loudspeakers hung. It's the church, said Adriano, you'll see, they're behind all of this. He muttered these words with downcast and mildly ashamed eyes. The center of the coffin-shaped grounds of the prison, on which all these old women seemed bent to converge (though I now saw a few other tourists, including four Germans in shorts, their knees crimson and their identical alpenstocks chopping the air), held a stumpy, open building made of cinder blocks and roofed with tin shingles. These looked molten in the sun. The old women here pressed thickly and strongly, they made forward movement difficult. You had to move at their numb, reverential pace or not move at all. We were gradually swept forward by this tidal motion, this erosive and mysterious motion, and I was able to see the building more clearly: it was a shrine, and within the gloom under its tin roof hundreds of squat candles burned and flickered. A name was lettered in orange paint on a wooden plaque hanging from the roof edge: SAN CRISTÓBAL.

The saint wore a purple robe. He was toweringly tall. The crude-cut hands, painted white, gripped the robe under its white collar. And from the collar up … I could not believe what I saw. A dog's head on the saint's shoulders. St. Christopher has a dog's head, Adriano whispered to me, I don't know why but you can look it up, I remember from school. As he spoke, from the loudspeakers mounted on the inner courtyard wall came a breathy recording of bells. The Dog Symphony: that's what it was, played on a carillon. The old ladies surged forward, one more human wave, and those in the first rank knelt and started to pray, they asked the saint to intercede for their dead sons and daughters, their dead sisters and husbands, on the perilous journey from death back into life, a journey like the journey our savior himself took. The prayer sounded rehearsed to me. Adriano said some priest had written it after the dogs first showed up. Or maybe not a priest at all, but some other authority—he couldn't remember. We'd reached the shrine itself now, buoyed by the flood of old women. A damp cold emanated from the wooden walls and from the plaster statue itself. Steel troughs filled with white candles stood before the concrete hexagon beneath the shrine.

Adriano was kneeling, now, fumbling up a candle from the trough and lighting it with his own (secular) matches. He didn't look at me, only at St. Christopher. The daylight once more rendered the flame almost invisible; but once he had placed it on the metal stands within the shrine it blazed a vivid orange, the color of the letters on the sign identifying the saint. I was now the sole person standing. Adriano muttered over his clasped hands, his eyes closed, rocking in the same cardiovascular rhythm as the old women. Around me the bent, hill-shaped backs, the gaudy and funereal kerchiefs, and the tolling song. Adriano interrupted his prayer to direct a guilty look at me, as though saying: What can I do? I don't know where my instinct to kneel and join him came from, but burgher adventurism demands that you engage in such displays. Then again, it could have been my natural cowardice. I did not take a candle but I did murmur, over and over, a curt prayer for Ana's safety as the soap-scented clothes of the old women rustled next to my ears. In the dim shrine, the candlelight spattered on a halo made of gold-painted plaster surrounding the canine head. You see, murmured Adriano, you see.

He and Fulvio lived, I learned, across from La Chacarita in a three-story house plastered and painted the color of tangerines. Over the meal he invited me to, which was neither lunch nor dinner, the brothers explained that they had grown up in this house and that they intended for their children to live in it after their own deaths. The teenage flower lackey was Fulvio's son, Hilário. He was more than a lackey: he was also a veterinary intern at a rural clinic. Adriano's daughter was named Luz Dar. Her cousin spent the whole meal casting lost, lustful glances at her breasts and eyes, at her sleek hair. She possessed a physical beauty (soft, snubbed melancholic chin; dewy irises; impeccable blackness behind her impeccable teeth) that stilled criticism and even observation. Her mother was dead. Her aunt, Fulvio's wife, kept a watchful eye on Hilário as we ate an enormous salad, dandelion greens and tomatoes, and then rice and roasted eggplants, along with sweating cans of Quilmes beer, which everyone in the Taquini family seemed to prefer to wine. They served no meat, for which Fulvio and his wife Odolinda apologized. Prices have never been so high, Fulvio said, and you already know the sad state of my business affairs.

Ojea Meat Distributors was, it seemed, a well-known meat company, though none of the Taquinis could explain why Ana might be working there. A simple transcription error by the Department, a malicious prank by the man who answered the phone: both were possible. Hilário mentioned a friend who had found his own phone number disconnected for no reason. The number no longer worked, he said, and he was in this way cut off from the world. Both Odolinda and Fulvio agreed that it had become hard to contact people since the epidemic. Odolinda said I shouldn't get confused, this was not the second coming of the dictatorship—whatever I might think, Rosas or Videla was nowhere to be seen in all this. She blamed Ana's absence on what she first called "national preoccupation," and then "civic preoccupation." We are all trying our best to understand what these dogs mean, whether they are, in fact … here she trailed off, as if she did not want to disagree with her husband and brother-in-law before strangers. It was too late, Fulvio was already shouting that she had no right to question the night-dog phenomenon, he worked too hard and she saw the evidence herself of what they were. We can't even afford fucking meat anymore, my love, Fulvio shouted, fists clenched. Odolinda shook her index finger near her husband's black nostrils and cried out: Don't tell me what to think, don't be an asshole.

After they both apologized for this outburst (first to me, then to each other, then to their family members), Adriano related the story of our journey to see St. Christopher. Fulvio spat, literally spat, each time Adriano mentioned the cynocephalic saint. His wife said: Don't be so theatrical, Fulvito. Her admonition warm, concealing her craterous laugh. Luz Dar said it was a shame they had knocked down the old prison. In a sense, said Luz Dar, you could call it our real heritage. Hilário fervently agreed, eyeing her breasts. Or they could have left it up, but as a museum, or they could have turned it into an office building. Anything would be better, said Fulvio. They could have built a dog crematorium. Luz Dar turned her (lightly cross-eyed) gaze to her cousin—who in a swift jerk removed his finger from his nose—and then to me. I did not want to weigh in on the dog question, I said, as a relative stranger. Adriano said his brother was right (I also kept quiet about his having lit a votive candle). Fulvio also did not know the exact date of the transformation of the carcel, and this troubled me far more than my having missed the news of the epidemic: the transformation of the Cárcel de Devoto into a shrine represented a massive loss to my profession. Odolinda blamed the University police cadres. They like keeping secrets for their own sake, she said. For example, I was trying to look up an old classmate of mine who works there, and they simply refuse to admit that she exists. They claimed her records were lost or stolen. It's part of our civic preoccupation, I suppose, she went on, but it's worrisome, as you yourself know, Mr. Pasternak.

No one could give me specifics about the epidemic. Fulvio said it was "the plague," in English. Adriano said no, it had been swine flu. Odolinda objected: That was the whole problem, they never identified it. Luz Dar and Hilário kept silent, slowly drinking the whiskey their fathers had poured them from the bottle I'd brought. The Taquinis hadn't lost anyone to the epidemic, I learned, which explained their unfamiliarity with it. Luz Dar, her voice raucous from the whiskey, said that someone she knew in school had an uncle who died. Hilário, who had grown more and more agitated during the conversation, was muttering something. His father said: Would you mind clarifying, Professor? No offense, Mr. Pasternak, but Hilário here often forgets that not everyone lives on his elevated plane.

Hilário looked at his father, wheezed, and said: It never happened, it's complete nonsense.

Fulvio said that as long as Hilário lived under his roof he would show respect, especially in the presence of company. Hilário responded in a calm voice: All the rules about politeness in the world, he said, won't change anything. The so-called epidemic never happened, it just didn't. And these dogs are not the dead, Dad, you're just using that as an excuse. Oho, said Fulvio, now you're an expert in business affairs! Quite a son I've raised. Hilário looked again at his cousin, whose gentle and crooked smile encompassed him, me, her father, her aunt and uncle, and the dandelion leaves in the cracked wooden bowl.

I don't claim to be any sort of expert, but I do know that if basic reality isn't worth suffering for then nothing is. He drained his glass and he too smiled, the ineffable smile that afflicts you in your youth, causeless and indeed humiliating. There you go again, Professor, said Fulvio. He sounded less sure in his use of the title. And rightly so. Academic work and reality stand in endless opposition. Who knows the eventual victor?

10.

AFTER THE MEAL, WHILE Fulvio and Adriano cleared the table and Odolinda scraped the crumbs from the cloth, Hilário and Luz Dar escorted me out onto their veranda. It overlooked Iturri (the Taquinis lived on Santos Dumont, near the corner). The floor planks and rails, to which orange plaques of eroded paint adhered, sang beneath us. Luz Dar and Hilário settled next to each other on a wooden swing bench; I leaned out over the railing into the night. The marijuana they smoked perfumed the otherwise scentless air, sweet and harsh. Luz Dar offered me the joint. I said no, I was too old for it. She and her cousin both chuckled. I peered down into the street. A navy-blue van was idling on Iturri, waiting with the precise, cold hunger of the state. My fears returned as I read the lettering: MAN'S BEST FRIEND SOCIETY.

Hilário said, through a cough, that they had something to do with the dogs, that they fed them or something. Luz Dar objected: Why would they feed them when everyone leaves meat out for them? Then maybe they sterilize them, Hilário muttered. It's a shame it's not possible to sterilize dogs at a distance. I think I read that in a story once. The van doors opened and three people in sky-blue uniforms got out, yawning and stretching. The cold hunger of the state, no doubt. Two carried round clubs made of white pine. The driver had a plastic bag filled with raw slabs of meat, which I pointed out to Hilário and Luz Dar. They didn't believe me at first but agreed, once they had come to lean beside me on the railing, that it must have something to do with the night dogs. I told them that I was going down to investigate, and they both sputtered out laughs. Are you fucking crazy, said Luz Dar, they'll arrest you. I pointed out that they were (judging by their uniforms) employees of the Department of Social Praxis, not members of the police force. She said it didn't matter, the cops let them arrest people, she'd seen it happen. You think people only stay inside at night because of the dogs? No, the University cops are out too, though they keep themselves well hidden. Her voice grew raucous and hardened. She seemed to be on the verge of tears. Just don't tell them you came from here, said Hilário, don't give them our address. The coal of the joint glowed and lit up his forehead, his thin eyebrows, and the liquid glare his beautiful cousin was directing at me.

I assured them I would not reveal any information. The promise seemed absurd as I said it. What authority did a group of dogcatchers have over human life? And I had to investigate, these were the vans from Avenida Zenz. I asked the two cousins to make my excuses to their parents for me. They said nothing, they smoked, that's all. I crept back inside, past a room (drowned in the blue glow of television) from which sweet, idle fraternal/matrimonial chatter drifted, interrupted by frantic outbursts (Boca was losing). In the kitchen, I found a back exit, a screen door. Beyond it juniper thickets hovered in the darkness. As I padded out onto the Taquinis' tiny lawn the creaking of the verandah swing slowed, slowed, ceased. The human voices in the upstairs parlor: these too faded. On the roof of the blue van two dark protuberances emerged, round and hard-looking, on thick stalks. I saw them as I was trotting over, screening myself with the juniper hedges, until I was near enough to observe the driver and the other two.

They were waiting. The meat-bag holder whistled a short phrase from the Dog Symphony. The club wielders whistled the next. All three chuckled, a glottal syncopated laugh. Possibly only one laugh but issuing from three throats. They choked it off before it could die naturally. The meat-bag holder eyed the van. On the lip of the rolled-down passenger window a well-molded arm in a sky-blue sleeve rested, the hand thin and strong, the nails blunt, a silver watch manacling the wrist. This fourth figure, not in uniform, was otherwise concealed by darkness. The juniper leaves pricked my face as I looked through the hedge gaps. The driver had opened her bag of meat and tossed the slabs out onto the asphalt of Iturri, where they landed with wet, osculatory noises. The two club wielders stood and stared toward Newbery, tapping their palms with their weapons. Faint, sparse barks and a narcotic rustling. I heard those familiar noises, along with the chiming the tags of the night dogs made, a chiming that grew louder, clearer and clearer, until I realized that a pack was ambling along Iturri, ready to join their fellows in the rush to La Chacarita. The meat that had been thrown into the street stopped the dogs and they began to chew with the same subtle care they displayed during my first observations.

The bag holder whistled. Two floodlights—the dark roof protuberances—burned to life. I had to shield my eyes with fingers made pink by the glare. When I was able to look at the street through the hedge again I saw four dogs, a Hungarian mudi, two whippets, and a juvenile rottweiler, all light-stunned, rags of meat dangling from their jaws. Blood tinted the whippets' adze faces. They stood shivering monastically as the club wielders went to work, striking the night dogs (almost regretfully) on their necks, just behind the bulges of their skulls. Each dog made a yelping whine as it went down. Once the dogs hit the asphalt, the club wielders—their escutcheon-shaped badges blank with light—struck them again across the skull. They had not killed the animals. I saw the pelts between the ribs of the lean whippets inflating and deflating. The club wielders threw open the rear van doors; the van's cargo area had been fitted with a cage—and in this cage sat and whined two other dogs, a beagle and a Weimaraner, on short chain leashes looped through dirty steel grommets screwed into the van wall. The club wielders tossed the unconscious dogs through the cage door. The taller one started to fasten new chains around their necks while the four were still dazed; the shorter one kept watch, club at the ready, on the beagle and the Weimaraner. The two dogs just stared. The bag holder came around to the cage with a clipboard and the hideous noise of writing arose. The taller club wielder said: Should we let her have a look at them now? The bag holder spat out her answer: Of course. The passenger door had already opened and the fourth figure was striding toward the oval zone lit by the flood lamps, striding and striding, the way a goddess strides across a field, a classical meadow flooded with light, for example. But before the woman had entered the oval of glare (she stood at its lip, rendered completely obscure by her proximity to the light) the shorter club wielder aimed his cudgel across the street at the juniper hedge concealing me and screamed: Hey asshole, what the fuck do you think you're doing?

I started to run as soon as the club wielder turned to face me. His wide cheeks grimy with stubble, afloat in the white light, adrift in the white light, aloft in the white light. A face I almost, in fact, recognized. I ran southeast on Iturri, so they would have to pull the van around if they wanted to chase me in it, I thought, and ran along Concepción Arenal toward the Parque Los Andes. There I could hide myself among Paraná pines, jacaranda, bryophytes, and the underbrush my namesake wrote about with such diarrheal eloquence. The empty streets aided me here. I was able to run with tremendous speed and ease because I faced no human obstructions, no hate-filled primate stare. The few dogs not already on Newbery paid me no mind; they either ate and drank or trotted on, their breathing velvety and punctuated by the modest chiming of tags. I wanted to warn them—but dogs do not speak and do not understand (or so I thought then). I said nothing. The wide-faced club wielder kept shouting behind me: Hey asshole! Hey asshole, get back here! His breath more and more ragged between each cry and his footsteps slowing, as if sleep were descending upon him. Victor, let him go, a female voice shouted. Fuck you, Victor shouted back, it's our job. Yet I heard only his footsteps. I realized these were the footsteps of a drunken man. The light, inconsequent stagger that expresses drunken inquiry. By the time I reached the lip of the park, I heard nothing at all behind me except for dimming shouts. He's just some asshole, let him run, I won't report you, and you have to admit he'll probably end up with us anyway. Under these circumstances this Victor ended his pursuit and I stumbled across a high, cracked curb into the park.

A car's ignition coughed and coughed, its motor wheezed and

thrummed, but the sound faded. Heading westward, I thought. I had almost regained my breath when two loud, at-hand, penitential sounds broke the leafy silence. Or rather the enleafed silence. Nine or ten yards from the ombu stand I was concealed in, near a crushed Quilmes can coated with oblique streetlamp glow, two brown mutts copulated vigorously. They kept up countermelodic howls, answered from near and far by howls and cries of their fellows. The night calling out to itself.

11.

MY RETREAT TO THE Parque Los Andes lasted for hours, until I was absolutely sure no University police remained nearby. I got back to the Pensión Vermesser exhausted, but I did not sleep. As morning arrived, gray and gold, I planned my return to campus. I called a taxi after I showered. The shower did nothing to alleviate my exhaustion. I greeted the impassive, deep-eyed driver with a stony nod. The distance between my head and feet seemed to increase and decrease without warning. My visual field fishbowled as I dragged the sandy detritus of another sleepless night from the corners of my eyes.

There was an official reason for my visit. The conference was proceeding at its normal pace, indifferent to my inane and hard-to-understand difficulties. I was due to participate in a session taking as its theme—here I also saw Ana's arranging hand—a subject that had fascinated me since I first entered my profession: the prison system of ancient Mongolia. Our most primal prison, our most supreme and invisible prison. Nothing but pits dug out of the Scythian earth supervised by a jailer on horseback. This system contained many surprising intricacies, more than enough material to keep a conference in vivid and rebarbative argument all day.

But I had no intention of showing up, no intention of running into the boy who looked like Che or a new set of student agitators. No, I went back to campus because I planned to enter Ana's office, to batter its door down if necessary, to break its chiropractic glass. Like all second-rate thinkers I played out two opposing scenes in my head.

The first: Ana alive and well, dressed in her simple and opulent clothing, laughing her hoarse, proleptic laugh at my concerns. You are adrift, Boris Leonidovich. Her normal rebuke. Thereupon I would chastise her, demand explanations for her absence, for the night dogs, for Sanchis Mira, for the Department itself, for Luxemburg, for the vans and for the occluded night I had plunged into.

The second: pure void.

Students flowed through the first floor of the social sciences faculty, the divisions between the tag wearers and those with naked necks yet more evident. Among them, security officers ambled and strutted, laughing and calling to each other. They held up their right hands and tapped their rigid fingers against the thumb, like a maw opening and closing, in time with the drumbeats of the Dog Symphony, now playing openly from radios students carried. The tag wearers mimicked this gesture, and I did as well. One officer caught me in his gaze. Not malicious, just curious.

The elevator door opened on eight and revealed a pristine wall, painted delicate blue. The floors no longer puce tile but sealed concrete, brutally gleaming (and tinted a deep night blue). Cool, sweet air moved lightly around me. The ventilation system had been improved as well. The blues, like sea and sky, accompanied me. The reception area was painted in the same two shades; the desk was new, it looked like ebony, and the visitor seats were Barcelona chairs, crisscrossed by leather straps.

They lacked the golden, rabbit-shaped label. I knelt on the cold floor to check. The east wing of the department, which did not contain Ana's office, stretched openly to my right. All the piled boxes, all the ossification, the shoes and laces, the spectacles, all these had gone. The hallway was vacant and utterly still. The doors, white, all stood open, and the odor of drying paint came from them. The black-and-gold names gone, though the rippling glass itself remained.

The west wing was under construction. Opaque plastic drop cloths hung from the ceiling, covering whole sections of wall. Here, the blue sealed concrete flooring had not been completely installed. A black seam divided it from the old puce tiling. Wooden sawhorses (stenciled DSP in sky blue) stood poised in their obscene manner along the walls. The air stank of ozone, fresh sheetrock, sawdust. The corridor stretched and stretched, growing dimmer and then fading into complete darkness: I passed through the hall, holding my lighter up as a torch. Either no electricity flowed here or the light fixtures had not been connected. Thuds and sawing noises, filtered by distance, colluded. The hall stretched much farther than I would have thought possible given the size of the building. Then again, I was suffering from a lack of sleep and a more general disorientation.

This corridor ended in a false wall made of sky-blue duvetyn and black metal struts; a door, also of cloth, was set into it. I opened it halfway, and the duvetyn door revealed more puce linoleum and planted upon it two legs in sky-blue pants with silver piping. I pushed harder, the panel swung fully outward. There, diagonally across this improvised exit, was Ana's office. Its door now stood ajar. Beyond, the room itself was empty, empty of everything except its old desk and faint squares on the walls.

I knew from a photograph she'd sent me what had once concealed these whiter patches: her own photographs of Juan Filloy, the only Argentine writer she respected (I always pretended I knew who he was to oblige her). The names on the doors to either side—ZINNY and DE GANDIA—gone. Ana's name still remained. In part. A lackey in sky-blue coveralls was effacing it with a rag and a glass beaker of solvent. The lackey wore a silver badge like those I'd seen flashing on the chests of the University police, but he was a lackey and nothing else, I could tell from his loose lower lip and dull stare. A short silver whistle on a leather thong hung from his loose-skinned neck. To the thong was affixed a golden label: GENUINE PAMPAS HARE. The silver whistle beat time against his concave chest as he spread solvent, rubbed, and clucked.

Ana's name was hard to eradicate. The lackey slid a putty knife from his pants pocket and began to chip at the gold-and-black paint. He chastised himself under his breath: Be careful, be careful, man, if you break this you'll be lower than shit. The noise of the knife against the glass, the insupportable and reverential noise—that's what made me finally speak. Excuse me, I said, but what are you doing? Such a question cannot be asked without sounding like you have just shambled on stage in a hideous, wooden play of domestic life. I knew that, yet I asked it. And even asked it again. The lackey looked at me. His knife stopped. Then he smiled a smile punctuated by a golden incisor and said: No need to worry, sir, it's all authorized. The knife scraped and scraped. More shreds of Ana's name flaked down to the tiling. The lackey went back to work with his rag.

I told him to stop, at once. He did, though he tried—by a series of blinks and grimaces—to mask his instant obedience as

82

surprise. This is fully authorized, sir, whined the lackey, I have full authorization. From whom, I said, making sure to be grammatical. From the boss, sir, he said. What boss, I said. From Dr. Sanchis Mira, he said. And where, I said, is Dr. Mariategui? The lackey shrugged. I heard she went on sabbatical. He returned to scraping and rubbing, and I walked past him into Ana's office. I caught an esteric whiff of his solvent. You can't go in there, he mumbled. I didn't respond. Even her scent—soap and sand—had dissipated. The lackey started whining again when I tore open Ana's desk drawers. You can't, sir, you just can't, moaned the lackey. The first one empty. In the second, gray grit. In the third: an enormous canine taken from a jaw, its root intact.

The lackey froze, rag aloft. The silence deep enough to reveal the slopping noise the solvent made against the sides of its jar. It doesn't concern me, it doesn't concern me, sir, I'm just here as maintenance, just doing construction, said the lackey. What is this, I shouted. My voice had taken on a nauseating, false-thunder rattle. The lackey dropped his solvent beaker. The glass splintered and an acrid, brief gust made my eyes water. The lackey was already running off down the hall. On the glass panel only the letter *E* remained.

In Ana's office, I found nothing else. There was one window, which overlooked from eight floors up a deep concrete service area crammed with sky-blue dumpsters holding construction debris. This view explained nothing. And neither did the white patches once screened by Filloy. My throat burned, stinging tears careened down my face. I wept into my hands.

A loud, curt noise startled me. The doorknob striking the bared office wall and leaving a lunar dent. Four legitimate representatives of sky-blue authority now crowded the open doorway. Two men and two women. Their faces gentle and, so to speak, nullified. Their apparent squad leader, a woman with sharp, high cheekbones and an inky, minuscule mole at the upper-right-hand corner of her rich lips, called back into the hallway: This is the one? It was Luxemburg, who had first accosted me in this hallway the night of the cocktail reception. Mr. Pasternak, said Luxemburg, put it down. Her command baffled me and I stepped forward to ask for clarification. Put it down, you fucking faggot, she said—her voice level and velvety—or are you deaf? She pointed at the tooth.

I told her I would not relinquish it. She took out her baton. Don't be an idiot, Mr. Pasternak, she said. I held the tooth. She struck my wrist with the baton once, lightly. My hand opened involuntarily and the tooth hit the puce tiles. Or: it struck eternity and its minor thump struck my tympanum. You were told to stay away, said Luxemburg. Her adjutants kept their eyes on me. I have no intention of leaving, I said. It's not up to you, can't you see that, you goddamn professors don't fucking understand anything, said Luxemburg. Her adjutants nodded three nods. I said, again, that I was not going anywhere, that I demanded to see Dr. Mariategui, my academic sponsor, my colleague, and my valued friend. The last phrase I shouted. My scoured throat ached. Jesus fucking Christ, said Luxemburg. She readied her baton. A leather cord dangled from the butt, and to this cord was affixed a gold label. I am going to ask you once more, said Luxemburg. I did not speak. In the silence, intestinal rumblings (to this day I believe they came from the lackey). Fuck you, then, said Luxemburg, as she brought her baton down on my right shoulder. On the cord label I saw the words, the three words, the three modulated, florilegial, black, slanted, English words.

12.

MY MOLAR LAY ON the nightstand. Yellow-gray, at rest. The footboard whippets slept, reflected in the dressing mirror. When I touched my eyebrows, my fingers scraped against bands of gauze. To the extent that I was present anywhere I was present in my bedroom (Violeta's), dusty and breezy.

Violeta herself sat at the desk, my useless papers rustling behind her back. She wore a pink oxford shirt and jeans; bare feet, darkly tanned. They dumped you on the sidewalk, she said. Then she held up two white slips of paper, grimy with writing. Dr. Mariategui left these, she said as she set them back down on the desk. The name stunned me, sickened me with hope. Then I remembered—she meant the Colegiales nephrologist, her old friend, and as she approached (and as her double appeared, stately and silent, in the dressing mirror) I read the name on the prescriptions: FELICIANO MARIATEGUI, D.M. Don't try to speak or move too much just yet, she said, internal medicine is not his specialty but he told me you need rest. She went on as my excavated molar stared at me. I've heard about cases like this, but I never thought they'd do it to a foreigner. She must have found the tooth beside me on the sidewalk and placed it on the nightstand, I thought.

Her strong palm across my forehead. It landed there, rested

there. Blunt morning light filled my open mouth. My tongue dead, heated, adhesive. In Violeta's right hand a glass filled with water and ice (also more blunt sunlight). The cold liquid hurt my throat but I gulped it down in the amphibious manner so frequent with Homo sapiens. Violeta told me I should be very grateful to Dr. Mariategui, who'd come late last night. A house call, Mr. Pasternak, in an era when house calls are utterly obsolete. I apologized. I attempted to apologize, I should say. The nephrologist had packed the wound in my gum with gauze. Violeta, who had managed to decipher my dry groans, told me to save my apologies: The Department of Social Praxis really had been getting out of hand, there was no denying it.

I passed out again. When I woke, the sun was well past zenith. Almost down. No longer shining into my mouth. I managed to get up, though the raw socket in my gum pulsed at every step. I picked the gauze pads free from my eyebrows. They came away smeared with tacky blood, and tore out hair as well. A green bruise shone under my right eye; another one, blue, shone on my left shoulder. The orderly, faint marks of a boot tread had not yet faded from my sternum, and my testicles were still swollen. The stream of water striking them in the shower caused a pain so intense and exquisite that I almost came, even as I cursed and spat. My urine streaking into the drain had a pinkish tint. The foam that spattered the sink during my dental ablutions was likewise pink.

After the shower, I gathered my passport and address book, and lined up my shirts monastically in my suitcase. My edited conference papers I discarded in the metal wastebasket next to the desk; then I retrieved them and tore them into strips, arranged them in the bathroom sink, turned on the fan, and burned them. The greasy, sour smoke made me gasp, and these gasps resurrected my bodily pain. I coughed up fine-misted blood. Blood soaked the dressing in my molar hole, soaked and colored it completely. The smoke cloud lingered, quivered, above the sink. I closed the door to conceal it, as one might tenderly close a door to contain a tender odor. It nonetheless leaked autumnally into my room as I packed my socks and my books. Chulkov's *General Theory* and the Apukhtin crushed my shirt collars, and then suitcase darkness crushed them, gravity crushed the closed suitcase, and God (who does not exist) crushed everything else.

I found Violeta in the living room, pouring water into the vase with two lilac stems, and told her I wanted to settle up. She led me to a small room off the kitchen, its door locked with two locks, and, at a narrow-legged black desk, using a black calculator that spat out white paper, she totaled my bill. It was much less than what it should have been, given her nightly rates. Perhaps her sense of dignity as a hotelier prevented her asking full price from a guest who had been arrested and beaten by the University police. We shook hands, hers still warm, still strong, and she asked if I intended to fly out that day. Yes, I said. I cannot recommend that, Mr. Pasternak, she answered, and then added that the airport was closed. For how long, I asked. Until tomorrow afternoon, most likely, she said, they made the announcement while you were asleep. My suitcase creaked, and with it my lungs. I asked when the next bus to Retiro Station left. A much better choice, Mr. Pasternak, she said, they mentioned nothing about trains. I knew where I wanted to go, to Chile, to Ana's homeland. Getting there was simple. The Belgrano line took you right over the border. And there I could dig up her father—he lived, I remembered, in Antofagasta, once a copper-mining town—and contact the police of Chile, famous through the contemporary southern world for their incorruptibility. Yes, I would announce, I would announce her death ... the term sickened me, but no other, nonperiphrastic term for death exists. Ana was dead, I assumed. I had already wept for her. And we never gave in to domestic theatrics. Reporting her death to any authority here was useless. But she retained Chilean citizenship, that I knew, and perhaps her onetime state might care enough—or at least despise its neighbor enough—to take notice.

On the bus to Retiro, the conductor looked at me over his shoulder. I saw his pitted cheeks and convict's stubble. Isn't everything possible, in the end? Even the black spire of Retiro station is possible. Only that spire is possible. Gallery lights, sulfur-yellow, poured forth from the upper facade. Students and pseudostudents leaned against the casemented bulwark facing Ramos Mejía. Around their necks nylon collars: black, green, blue-and-white checked, red, a few tangerine. Attached to the collars tin tags shaped like crossbones. These chimed at each student gesture, each student breath. In their numbers the tags could be heard above the taxis, the bass blares of bus horns. Two sets of steel bowls sat before the north and south entrance arches, in which marble-lit darkness gathered. Slicing this darkness: arms and legs. I kept my gaze on the dim cement as I crossed the pavement skirt and inhaled the powerful student smell—sweat, soap, and smoke. My raw eyebrows hurt and my bruises ached; I paused over each garbage can to empty my mouth of bloody spittle. But the security officers didn't notice me, their sky-blue limbs went on slicing up facticities and shards. Despite their presence, the station appeared to be open and functional.

Within, the student smell overpowered the last remnants of coagulated blood in my nose and pharynx. Here they leaned against the walls, sat on the floor. Their shadows flickered near the short corridors leading to the restrooms. At the doors of shops, near the electronic ticket kiosks, and outside the currency exchange they formed knots of five and six and held empty metal bowls up to passersby, who threw change and paper money into them. The security officers did nothing to dislodge them. The students pulled out apitos, referee whistles, or small dog-shaped plastic toys (you pressed your lips to their tails) and blew short, shrill notes to greet each officer as he or she passed. Other whistle-bearing students heard and responded. The blasts propagated themselves through the shallow nave of the original station building, which dates to the presidency of Victorino de la Plaza. The officers smiled faintly at the whistlers and passed onward; as I was spitting blood into a trash can the owner of a cart selling fried meat slabs tapped an officer's shoulder, begged her to intervene. These fucking kids are driving me crazy, ma'am, he said. But she jerked away from his touch. The meat vendor suffered so-called state paralysis. Cartographic grease stains enriched his apron.

To reach the platform from which the Belgrano-line trains departed, I had to pass through the stone building pierced with whistles. All the stores and even the food-sellers had set out meat and water bowls. The disappointed fried-meat vendor was, in fact, beginning to lay fresh slabs down and to pour fresh water from a plastic bottle. He knelt by his bowls, head lowered, eyes almost shut. The vast doors leading to the platforms flamed up before me, filled with sunset, orange, reddish, umber—in general furnace-like. A raft of trains was boarding:

the announcements rippled through and over each other, trains for Coronel Pringles, Mendoza, Tucumán. The granular human flow ramified. The students stayed where they were against walls and near doors. Security officers continued to amble and pace. My train was not due for another forty-six minutes.

Other travelers loped alongside me, hushed and polite, gazing at the dark floor tiles (as if measuring distances). As I (we) neared the doors, as the curved glass roofs above the platforms gleamed and the rail yards extended their extensibility, the stream thickened and hardened, slowed. Our progress stopped. The segmented glass glowed, in a chitinous fashion. Security officers trotted from traveler to traveler, asking soft-voiced questions. They followed no visible pattern, moving as the winds of the state blew them and wearing their blinding smiles. Dental smiles. No other kind is known to taxonomic science. A male officer leaned in to ask a woman in an indigo dress with white flowers standing near me: Is your destination domestic or foreign? She answered domestic, and the officer touched her elbow. The woman sped off, toward a widening group gathered near a newspaper kiosk. The officer's nameplate read TUCHOLSKY. His face was long and ended in a roundish vertex like a rat's. I readied myself for his question. But he did not ask it. He showed me his upper teeth—hypertrophied, again like a rat's—and drifted away.

Tendrils budded from the domestic train group. The tendrils became thick trunks of their own. A vegetal process took place in metaphor. Also reality. Each trunk was a line; each line formed, I saw, according to destination: Coronel Pringles, Mendoza, Tucumán. At the head of each line an officer in sky blue. The travelers leaving Argentina were far fewer in number. I was one, an old man skillfully peeling an orange with his thumb—the rind came away in a single unbroken skein—was another, and a young family, all short, wide-shouldered, and black-haired, mother, father, and daughters, formed the third and last group. The security officer who took my initial information (her name plaque read MAUTHNER) handed me off to another officer (GIEHSE). Giehse wanted to know my destination country. I told her Chile. She held my passport up, to compare my photo with my face, and asked me what had happened. I answered with a brief lie. Two guys had beaten me up in Balvanera because they thought I was looking at their girlfriends, I said. I don't blame you for leaving town, Giehse answered. I asked what the next step was, and if she thought I would make the next train. That is not up to me, Mr. Pasternak, said Giehse, you'll have to speak to our exit visa section administrator. She pointed her impeccable finger (the sunset blazed through it) toward the far end of the concrete platform where the passengers would wait to embark. It was completely empty except for a line of brown notice boards and a sky-blue hexagonal shed at the northwestern tip.

The old man kept his eyes on his orange and the squat family glanced downward as I passed. They were bound for Bolivia, that's what the wife told the officer questioning them, her voice low and measured. I looked behind me, at the everyday void, in which Giehse stood. I took one step back, then another, a third. I'd almost passed her, I was close enough to smell her grassy perfume, when she gripped my upper arm. Is there some problem, Mr. Pasternak, asked Giehse. I said that there was no problem, just that I thought I had forgotten my razor back at my hotel. And which hotel was that, said Giehse. La Veneziana, I said, I always stay there. I know the hotel, said Giehse, it's a quality establishment. You don't need to worry, you can let them know you left something and they'll send it along to Chile. A line of officers now divided this section of the station from the central hall, questioning and directing departing passengers to the appropriate group, and the domestic travelers' conclave knotted, swelled, darkened. I envied them and their Coronel Pringles, I envied them and their Tucumán. Mr. Pasternak, said Giehse, I'm afraid once you've reached this point you have to continue, otherwise we'll need to process you all over again and you'll miss your train. Her fingertips rustled against my windbreaker. Yes, the tones, the suave tones. I didn't move. I watched the domestic travelers. Mr. Pasternak, said Giehse, is there some issue you'd like to tell me about?

I turned to face the blue shed, and Giehse released my arm. You have nothing to worry about vis-à-vis your possessions, Mr. Pasternak, she said as I walked, continuing past her into the warming emptiness. The metal and glass vaults covered most of this platform, but my destination lay on the exposed section, at the extreme end. I was the only traveler on the Belgrano line, it seemed; no one had been processed before me. My footsteps scraped against the porous, faintly blue concrete of the platform. The sun fragmented on the shining roofs of the shantytown spreading eastward from the bus parking lot across Mugica, spreading and taking root beneath the Arturo Illia overpass. Radios and speakers blared there as well, but not the strains of the Dog Symphony, I noted: soccer announcers, droning old songs from Mexico, advertisements for soap and the lottery. This mild cacophony went unheard by any security officers. None stood with me on the platform. The Department knew none would be required, that all the travelers would conduct themselves like obedient lackeys from that point onward; they would march across the concrete, enter the dark shed, and kneel (even if they remained standing).

I made my way toward the blue kiosk. At first it looked empty, so I dawdled, I watched the other travelers, I smelled the air—lilac, iron, and rotting trash—and I listened to the creaking of my suitcase. The kiosk was not empty. A human or allegedly human figure stood within, perfectly motionless and erect. A stooped man, I saw, wearing a white shirt, the collars and cuffs grayed by clerical grime. His clean naked scalp, ivory with age, defied the whiteness of the shirt as well; his hexagon within the kiosk was empty except for his wheeled stool and a sky-blue safe the size of a North American mailbox. I approached him, suitcase sighing (like the breath in my lungs). I crossed the wooden threshold (also sky blue). He asked for my passport, and his molars flashed.

As the security officer had done before him, he held it up, looked from it to my face, looked from the digestive pupil of the state to the digestive octagon, and then said: You look like you've lost weight, Mr. Pasternak. He asked me my destination, and after I told him, he asked why on earth I wanted to go to Chile. A smile, as ivory as his pate, appeared as I babbled out an answer in earnest: I had always wanted to see the famous town Antofagasta, I said, due to my great amateur interest in copper mining, the town's historical industry. Sweat burned in my scabbed eyebrows, and the clerk released a dusty laugh or curt belch. You do not strike me as the type to be interested in historical main industries, said the clerk. I assured him I was, that while I had come to Buenos Aires for a conference I had a strong personal interest in all historical industries, especially copper mining. The clerk stroked his sternum (above the heart) with a placatory hand, which resembled an inflated sterile glove. I started to assure him again that I was a lover of industry, but he interrupted me: One moment, Mr. Pasternak.

He turned and opened the safe with three deft movements of his swollen hand and tossed my passport into the thick darkness it contained. I objected, but the clerk repeated his injunction: One moment, sir. He shut the safe. On the wooden lip that served as his clerical counter were two objects, a (sky-blue) telephone and a dense-looking registry (bound in sky-blue leather). Each page frail enough to mildly transluce as he turned it with a licked, leaden finger. Human voices rose and fell in the warm, scented evening. No train had yet arrived but this did not disturb the general, jovial calm of the other travelers, those standing on the platforms to the west, beyond the clerical hexagon containing Pasternak and dust motes. Here too the Department had placed no barriers to burgher behavior. Here too they counted on innate lackeyism to keep travelers from deviating, from violating procedure. And the insult, well, it pierced me more and more, crushed and insulted me more and more. I was swaying, now, my eyes on the endless kiosk floor tiling, my pupils twitching as they counted off: one, two, three.

The clerk finished leafing through the registry. He glanced up at me and fell into a swift, azure silence, an azure silence in which he glanced at the sky-blue phone on the lip of his kiosk. Stay where you are, please, he said in his dry, precise voice, I will return your document once we have finished here. You understand that I need to contact my superiors, said the clerk. And the void glared from his mouth, cloaking his molars. The clerk cried out in pleasure as he located the entry in the register he had been seeking. His grayish hand settled on the blue, curved receiver. He lifted it, showing me once more his vacuous, me-phitically twinkling mouth.

In the filthy tunnels of memory, to my eternal guilt, I recalled that Ana was dead, gone from this life, gone at the hands of, gone at the mustache of. I recalled this only then despite ear-lier claims, only then, only now, now, now. Only as that black-mouthed clerk fondled the receiver. I rushed up to the waist-high partition between us and drove my fist into that starry nothing.

The clerk's teeth tore open the sticky, serpentine wound across my knuckles left by a baton blow. His shoulders and head collided with the rear kiosk wall; he himself, or his soul, or his colon whined. I struggled over the wooden lip, I entered the choked hexagon within the kiosk, and I kicked the supine clerk in the face, I kicked him once, twice, three times, four, five. Each blow revived my bodily pain, each blow sent sweat stingingly into my open brows. The clerk piped whistling cries as sleep or shock dragged him down. He was old, but I do not apologize. He had the immortal Department as a conceptual parent, and a Department voice now spoke through the fallen receiver: Hello? Hello? Blood from the clerk's mouth smudged my wingtip, and a gold incisor lay on the blank floor tile.

I looked through the three windows to my left and observed: no visible disturbance. The travelers gathered on the domestic departures platform, the squat family floated on the Bolivia platform, and the old man was still peeling his orange. To my east a fence, an empty, weed-broken concrete expanse (toward Ramos Mejiá, this expanded into a parking lot), another double set of empty platforms and tracks, Padre Carlos Mugica, and the spike-shaped southern tip of the shantytown, its roofs now dark. I let go of my sighing suitcase as the voice on the phone continued to chirrup. I checked the other platforms and the station exit again: no security officers swarmed out to arrest me, nothing at all except the aborted and dental platform lights. The distance to earth from this platform was negligible, about five feet, so—I leaped down. No one, I realized, could see me. No track workers, no signalmen paced this section, and I had a clear path to the fence. Cold and greased beneath my fingers, like the fence at the meat distribution company on Zenz. I was contemplating how best to climb over, when I saw a tear, half-concealed by a clump of melic, its furry stem tips nodding in the breeze. Gravel spattered as I worked my way through, and a sharp-ended cut fence link tore open my windbreaker, but not my skin.

The Department's arrogance, its grand insult, resounded. I saw no one, no one at all in the parking lot, the cars (all white) contained no one and no attendant's booth shone out at the front. Through the silence, the silence that always blankets the zone around train yards, the kiosk phone went on chirping. Even the mingling announcements from within Retiro reached my ears. I kept trotting along in the twilight, not too fast, toward the unwatched gate in the fence facing Ramos Mejiá. Above it curled a stunted, scentless jacaranda.

13.

THE CITIZENS OF THE shantytown—in effect, the truest porteños—kept late working hours. This I observed for myself.

From ornament boxes or tangled piles, they lifted watch buckles, metal studs for trimming handbags, rolls of sateen lining, golden rabbit-shaped labels reading GENUINE PAMPAS HARE. A whole family in one house, mother, father, and triplet sons, all three faces stained red by a repetitive birthmark, sat at a card table and worked; in another, an old man and an old woman—who might have been siblings or husband and wife—engaged in the same labor as their radio blared out a Chopin barcarolle (I knew because my friend and colleague whistled phrases from it if her fury prevented her from speaking). Many of the shantytown dwellers, regardless of their age, wore jeweler's loupes, which lent an inexplicable and utterly sinister element to their appearances. Euclidean scissors flashed in the dense, yellowed light, needles leaped and thread followed, pulled along with a nineteenth-century strength.

And in every house, too, I saw the same piles of objects next to the worktable. Stiff, hairy polygons, in many cases with the skin over the skull and the tail attached. The shantytowners worked with such speed that I saw the hides fully transformed: the pelt of a former fox terrier (I thought) was sliced up in threes and made into watchbands, and with the skin that once covered a mastiff the old couple sewed a handbag. They caught me spying but didn't seem to care, they both grinned and waved, and called out: Good evening, sir. Then they sewed a clasp onto the handbag's gaping mouth, set it aside, and picked up another skin. Ink-black and softly shining.

As befits a sufferer in a dream, I had no specific idea where I was, only that I was heading northwest toward my goal: the American Consulate on Colombia just south of Avenida de Libertador. Streets here, however, had no names. The lanes and alleys lacked public lighting as well. Most illumination came from within the houses. The shantytown dwellers filled the narrow streets, moving from house to house, asking their neighbors how the work was going, reporting on their own "progress"—that's the term they used repeatedly. A young man, tall and wedge-shaped, wearing an amethyst-purple tracksuit with the name KATALIN-SKI lettered across the shoulders, seemed to be organizing this procedure. He looked in almost every window, smiled, waved, and reminded the dwellers: There's a truck coming every day this week, so don't worry if you have too much for the A shipment. He even said hello to me. Smiling, silent children, boys and girls alike, weaved left and right, pushing wheelbarrows full of skins (heading southeast) or finished goods (heading northwest, like me). Katalinski paid close attention throughout all his greetings and unctuous encouragements to the wheelbarrow bearers, nodding, making hard, curt gestures with a finger, and the kids obeyed with a speed that unnerved me.

Above us was the Illia overpass; the shantytown dwellers had continued building without interruption beneath it; here exterior bulbs dangled more abundantly than before, to compensate for the shadow cast by the overpass and the concrete pylons supporting it; here the lanes widened and wheelbarrow drivers traded loads of finished goods for loads of skins. Around us children furiously unloaded and reloaded wheelbarrows, and they whistled or shouted greetings at the man in the amethyst tracksuit. Katalinski circled and roved through the crowd. I cut out from the overpass shadow, he darted across my path, gave me a sour glance, and vanished behind a cubical house. I walked up a gentle rise. Beyond the low roofs, beyond the railyard, the first greenswards of Recoleta appeared, the Parque Thays and the United Nations plaza, resembling black lakes. Along Mugica, alone and loud, a blue van coursed, and I crouched next to a house where an adolescent woman held a dachshund skin up to the grimy bulb hanging from her ceiling, ignoring me.

In each sharp shadow I saw a security officer, I saw Luxemburg. Hard-beaten dirt spread emptily and tawnily before the doorways. No bowls, no meat, nothing. Blue plastic-walled outdoor toilets (surrounded by clouds of night-born flies) stood in for interior plumbing; filthy rivulets ran down the center of many streets, even down the main streets—children and adults alike plashed through them, spattered in graying muck up to the ankle, up to the knee. The dwellers, too, kept close together, moving in streams or swarms.

Two wheelbarrows collided. The children pushing them, a boy and a girl in identical jeans and T-shirts advertising the Ojea Meat Company, started to swear at each other, swear and laugh. I collapsed against a stack of tractor tires in fear, my knees bent, the porous, stinking rubber struck my right cheek. The girl was heaping up the purses that had slipped from the boy's wheelbarrow, and the boy was arranging the skins that had fallen from the girl's (by size, largest to smallest, and with shocking speed). They both kept looking at me as Katalinski had done: with dark, soured glances. After they'd finished loading up the purses once more, they did not seize the wheelbarrows and drive them away but embraced each other, whispering and looking at me. Katalinski appeared and tousled their hair, and they forgot all about me, it seemed. My fear receded. I staggered past the stacked tires, staggered along in the street muck, as the light, heavy tread of Katalinski continued to resound behind me. My lungs burned from the few miles I had walked and from the effort I expended in my assault on the clerk. The long lane stretched into the gray-green darkness, where the houses lost their distinct outlines, where the proleptic haze of the parks was soon to begin. Behind me open laughter and mockery rang out. The shantytown dwellers chuckling (I assumed) at my hesitation. A smeared shout rose and died, too quickly for me to determine its meaning. The word "azogue," that was the single word I knew it had contained—in that shimmered a sinister threat. Like the faint train whistles punctuating the radio noise.

There he is, there he is. Two voices shouted, two juvenile voices. I turned to face my accusers and the brightness made me squint, but I saw them: the boy and girl from the earlier accident, now surrounded by a crew of adult men and women, all carrying white, knob-ended objects. That's him, said a red-haired woman, bending down to speak to the girl. Yes, yes, that's him. Without speaking another word, the knot of people moved toward me. I started to run. Look at that guy go, a voice shouted, maybe it's not him. I broke left and right as often as I could, to confuse my pursuers, whose footsteps spattered in the dust and muck, along with their laughter and cries: I think he went this way, no, no, he's over near the Alonsos, near the depot. The paths here were filled, as well, with wheelbarrow drivers, and they all broke into a unitary shout when I cut through their ranks: It's him, it's him, over here, hey, you guys, he's here. These wheelbarrows all bore finished goods, and they all appeared to be moving to the shantytown's northwest point, as I was. Blood leaked in two streams from my torn brow into my mouth.

The polyphonic noise of my pursuers accompanied me. They hadn't yet caught up with me. I stumbled into a massive thoroughfare, dead straight, at the end of which I saw the houses subside and the named streets begin. Here, the rivulet deepened into a brook. I had to dash through it to keep away from my pursuers thronging to my left and right, who shouted out that I was there, I'd arrived, come on, I was there; or else they stopped in their tracks and pointed at me, their grins subtle but visible. As I neared the limit of the shantytown, my dread and my hope increased. I could no longer see or hear my pursuers. The wheelbarrow drivers did nothing to hinder my progress. Like all children, they enjoyed cruelty, and it was far more cruel to let me run than to stop me. Between the shantytown edge and the short bridge Mugica passed beneath spread a band of dry, dead ground. The moonlight on it picked out the metal rails of the train tracks crossing that empty zone. Now my hope bested my dread. I spat out blood and swiped my sleeve across my forehead.

At first I didn't perceive the blow that felled me. Only as I stumbled into the tracks did I understand I had been struck down. My pursuers formed a wedge, now headed by Katalinski. Almost everyone was holding a club; the man who'd thrown his at me smiled smugly, his club lay, I saw, near my right foot. A bone, a dog's femur bone. Since I could not stand, I examined it: the joint end had been drilled out and filled with lead. The warm wood of the ties pressed against my spine, and the cold steel of the rails pressed against my skull. Katalinski wore a broad, flat smile: the man who'd thrown the club at me widened his smirk. My other pursuers hooted and whistled, clapped and cheered as I tried to force myself to my feet. A long thrumming note from the rail caressed my scrotum and bowels. Go the fuck back to the University, shouted the club thrower. We have everything under control here. Katalinski's smile hardened, vanished, and an attenuated, obliterating noise that I believed at first was a scream, my own torn voice, burst forth. Not a scream but a train's warning whistle. My legs like all dead limbs possessed great dead strength, and so I tossed myself onto the earth beyond the track and dragged myself away. I even managed to bring the bone. The train's headlamp was extinguished, a human figure leaned from an aperture in the engine cab, and the cars thundered past, a conjoined and oblong darkness. The passing train shielded me from my pursuers, true, but even its ordnance-like sound could not blot out their laughter.

I had just gathered my breath when hot light, a palpable force, struck my neck and ears. It came from behind me, it revealed the last cars of the thundering train (painted deep green, their doors open to the night streaming past) and my pursuers standing on the other side of the tracks, grinning, panting, their brows damp and their eyes indifferently clear. I turned my back on them to find the source of the light, but I could not, it blinded me. I stumbled to the concrete. Katalinski screamed: Come and get him, we found you a stray. His colleagues echoed the cry. My eyesight had returned, though orange nebulosities bloomed and died across my visual field. In the shadows along Salguero, I saw a night-blue van, with the sky-blue words MAN'S BEST FRIEND SOCIETY painted on its side panels.

Security officers were climbing out. One I recognized: Luxemburg. Her cap could not fully conceal her rich hair. Who's in charge here, she shouted across the tracks to my pursuers. I am, cried Katalinski, and like I said you can see we found a stray for you. And please tell Olegario to make sure the fucking truck is on time in the morning. Luxemburg nodded, assured him she would. Is there anything else, ma'am, said Katalinski. You can go, she said. Yes, ma'am, Katalinski said. The redheaded woman next to him cried: Hey beautiful, what are you doing on that side, you should be over here with me. Mr. Pasternak, said Luxemburg. I didn't answer. Mr. Pasternak, she repeated. The van driver (did I recognize him?) rushed up, overtook her. Answer her, he said. I raised the bone club. Mr. Pasternak, said Luxemburg. She drew her gun. Get on your knees, she said, put your hands on your head. I knelt and I placed my hands on my hot scalp.

14.

I USED TO DRINK but I had to give it up, Luxemburg said. Her colleague chuckled. Fuck you, he replied, you never gave it up. I gave it up in theory, said Luxemburg, which is all that's required. The rearview mirror showed me their rigid grins. I did recognize her companion: Victor, the boy from the lecture hall. The student who had assaulted me and the female shouter. He was also wearing a sky-blue uniform now, and was armed with a gun, a baton, and a whistle. His nameplate read KLEM-PERER (it appeared, reversed, in the mirror, and I was able to decipher it). Luxemburg lifted one hand to show she meant no harm. Don't worry, Professor, you have nothing to fear, she said, not from him and not from me. Luxemburg you can't trust, said Klemperer. She has Gypsy blood. That's not what we call them anymore, said Luxemburg.

A cage was fitted to the rear of the van's cargo area. Brown stains streaked the floor beneath it. Luxemburg asked if I was cold. I told her no. She twisted and leaned into the rear cabin and raised a thermos to my lips, lifting it so I could drink. It did not contain coffee, as I expected, but juice, papaya juice. To my own surprise, I drained the thermos without stopping. She held it up the whole time, Luxemburg watching me drink. You need to keep your energy up, she said. Klemperer slapped the radio.

Luxemburg warned him not to break it or it would come out of his pay. Between them, on the front floor of the cab, a shovel lay rattling as we drove. We don't earn much, she said to me, smiling slightly, we do this work for other reasons. Speak for yourself, said Klemperer.

They didn't touch me, they didn't beat me, they simply hand-cuffed me and lifted me from the ashen earth near the train tracks into the backseat of the van, locked the door, and started driving. I was too tired to respond with anything but compliance. Without a word, we passed into the null greenery that surrounds and insulates the southern capital. Klemperer, at last, found two radio stations that were broadcasting clearly and switched between them, news and jazz, back and forth, until Luxemburg told him to stop, to pick a fucking station and stay there. Klemperer ignored her and asked me, instead, if I wanted a cigarette. This I accepted. See, Professor, no hard feelings, said Klemperer. He twisted back—eyes on the road, asshole, said Luxemberg—and shook one from his pack. The golden word MACEDONIA encircled the filter. I took it in my lips. Luxemburg lit it. Smoke streamed toward the open windows.

The night dogs had gone, yes, but very few humans appeared on the streets. Almost none in the scrawny suburb we passed through. The buildings low and red, the pedestrians all old, neatly dressed in a clerical, timid way, their hair white or non-existent, the outlines of their bodies blurred with age. At every door, with no exceptions, meat and water bowls and shrines above them. The shovel rattled on.

This is all going to be over soon, Professor, said Klemperer, I promise, so just try to relax. I'd offer you weed but we can't smoke it on the job. Sudden laughs choked me, stopped me from answering. I closed my mouth, clamped my teeth together, I rocked on the jump seat. Now, Professor, there's no need for that, Klemperer went on. Luxemburg said: Can't you see he's upset, asshole? Klemperer, his eyes canine and moist in the mirror, apologized. I didn't mean anything by it, Professor. Ruts opened in the road beneath us. Luxemburg's black boots reflected the empty, tree-edged sky flowing outside, in the so-called world. Dampness leaked through my shirt. He's all sweaty, said my benefactor. No kidding, said Klemperer. And it's going to be a hot one today, right, Professor? Luxemburg was lifting another thermos. I leaned forward; she took the butt from my lips, and replaced it with the thermos. This one held cold, sweet tea, and I drank it with the same speed I had consumed the papaya juice. A news announcer started to speak, a woman with a sculptured voice, but Klemperer switched back to the jazz station before she could finish a word.

An abrupt chain-link fence rose from the auburn dirt, and Klemperer slowed. When we stopped, Luxemburg got out and opened the door for me, watched me step down. I stumbled as I made contact with the earth, and she grabbed my upper arm to keep me from falling. Klemperer, without preamble, climbed out and unzipped his fly. The air smelled like rue and cortaderia, as well as asphalt and exhaust. DSP signs (sky-blue letters on white) bolted to the fence rattled in the wind. In the fence, a gate, on the gate a padlock, beyond the gate, with no visible preamble, a beaten dirt track began in the tangle of rue. I could see nothing beyond the waving plants except taller grasses deeper into the field. Klemperer's urine splashed luxuriously.

In the van, a service radio chimed. Luxemburg leaned in through the passenger window to answer it. Static blurred what her fellow officer or superior was saying (I imagined, stupidly, that it was Sanchis Mira, I summoned up that mighty mustache) but she understood it or pretended to, and she assented. Yes, roger that, she said. Roger that, cried Klemperer, as he shook his dick (I'd turned my head to keep it out of my vision, but I saw his foreskin sliding back into place over his broad, bright-purple glans). Luxemburg trotted around the blue van, now carrying the shovel, her whistle thumping lightly against her chest. She unlocked the padlock and Klemperer motioned me to walk forward. I had reached the door when he said, Okay, that's good. Luxemburg came up behind me. I thought she was going to hit me with the shovel, but instead I heard its blade strike the earth and felt her fingers on my wrists. The handcuffs opened. Klemperer told me to pick up the shovel and get walking. I didn't obey, at first, I was staring at the waving leaves of a cinquefoil plant next to his spreading urine. Come on, Professor, get going, said Klemperer. He unholstered his gun. The metal sighed against the leather. Two wet spots darkened the gusset of his sky-blue pants. The serrated, silvered leaves trembled. The dust soaked up his urine.

Klemperer, as he shuffled along behind me, hummed a phrase from the Dog Symphony. More than twelve hours had passed without my hearing it, I calculated as I inhaled the sweet, high smell of the rue, the grass growing among its stalks, the earth itself. As I followed the single, sinuous path, I imagined we were approaching a facility, one that resembled the Parque Presidente Sarmiento, with its swimming pool (I don't know why I thought there would be a swimming pool but I did, I unquestionably did) and its bizarre red-brick colonnade. I called over my shoulder (the shovel's still-cool edge brushed my face) to ask Klemperer where we were going. He said not to worry, that this was Department property and no one would bother us, we'd be finished here in a few minutes. The grasses rose higher and higher, and I saw that we'd reached a deep thicket of Cortaderia selloana, the famous Argentine pampas grass. Watch out for the Pampas hares, cried Klemperer. I laughed, and my laugh vanished like smoke under the faultless sky. No clouds, no birds, not a single plane visible, just a vacant, hard blue that the tips of the tallest grasses seemed to touch.

Let no one say that Pasternak regards himself as above manual labor. I had a shovel. This meant: digging. The ground sloped, this I knew too, though I could not tell if it sloped upward or downward. At times it seemed we were ascending and at times descending. The unchanging, smoothed sky prevented me from developing any real idea. Klemperer called me over; he kept the gun ready. The grasses closed above us, only a narrow, oblong strip of sky could be discerned.

I used the shovel edge to chop down the harder stems blocking our path and Klemperer called out approvingly. That's good thinking, Professor, no wonder you did so well in academia. He understood, of course, what the shovel meant to me, what I knew it to mean. He understood as well the absurd and obscene fantasies that it inspired. And he regarded these fantasies as nothing. He even began to whistle again, to feign absorption in his whistling, rigidly keeping his face averted from me, the shovel in my hand, alive with sun as his whistles reached an intolerable fluidity and pitch—his mastery of the music was incredible; a born whistler, a man whose whistling outstripped all his other talents. He did not stop whistling as he unzipped again and started to piss. This time he fully turned his back, lifting his chin skyward and whistling. His cap fell to the grass and revealed the crown of his head. A nude pink spot among the luxurious hair surprised me. And I did nothing, I hacked away at a thick stem with my shovel. The shaft raised welts on my palm, and these had already begun to blister. I watched Klemperer piss, I heard the splashing urine form a counterpoint to his mighty whistling, and the grave, the earth, closed over my head, Pasternak—that's what you thought.

I didn't recognize the swift grayish object that flashed out of the thicket. Neither did Klemperer. Its speed so great, its presence so numinous, that he gave a small, sweaty cry of terror and leaped back. The gray creature scurried between his legs and he tried to dodge again, but this time he missed his footing and fell to the grass. I moved before I knew I was moving. That's how I overcame the insult. That's the only way. Pasternak leaped forward and struck Klemperer's face with the shovel.

The gun fell from his hand. He whistled, he whistled some more, yes. A whistling cry. My first blow opened a deep gash across his cheeks and nose, and I saw within the gash the pearly darkness that had also flowed from the torn lips of the woman Klemperer struck. The second blow destroyed Klemperer's left eye. His right eye trembled and rolled as he thrashed beneath me. The third blow (and here my transcription becomes more precise) penetrated his skull, and gelatinous gray matter spattered my hands and face. Which is to say Pasternak's hands and face. Which is to say the face and hands of Boris Leonidovich. Then Klemperer stopped whistling, but I did not stop striking. I raised the shovel and struck again, again, again. With each blow more pearly darkness flowed upward into the light, with each blow this darkness diluted itself, until I could no longer discern the difference between this pearly darkness and the hard sunlight. Klemperer soon stopped moving entirely. The mild, broken hitching of his chest ceased. I kept striking. His skull began to lose its structure. Now bright arterial blood decorated my arms and my face. Droplets flew into my mouth.

The gray creature, the Pampas hare, had observed all this. When I was finished with Klemperer, I raised my eyes to find it crouched, staring, its eyes fiery yellow, its pupils deep, velvety black, its paws and belly cloud-white. I dropped the shovel. The hare stayed there, utterly still, and then darted away. I watched its massive hind legs, its long ears (one notched from a predator's bite), and its flame-like tail as it vanished. After that, quiet. No more whistling, no more pissing. No sound at all from Pasternak, which is to say me. I picked Klemperer's gun from where it had fallen. A Browning; as noted, I knew its design. I thumbed the safety off—he had not yet done this, so great was his confidence in the departmental insult and its success—and leaned back against the unbroken stretch of grass thicket. The stiff stems supported me. The problem was clear. Luxemburg. I could not at first decide on the best way to deal with her. If I waited long enough she would arrive but she would arrive suspicious. If I fired a shot, to simulate my own execution, that would provide me with philosophical camouflage, and I could creep back along the path we had broken and attempt to shoot her by the side of the road. That was much riskier, as I could not guarantee my approach would be silent. The method I settled on was simple and stupid. I walked back toward the fence, pushed myself into a deep, dense area of the grass thicket halfway between the gate and the zone where Klemperer lay, and started shouting Luxemburg's name.

I didn't have to wait long. The sun above passed from the green tip of one grass stalk to the white panicle of another. Then Luxemburg's rapid, even footsteps began to rustle, as they had that evening we first met in the history department's evacuated hallway. She had her gun drawn and raised and she was not running, she cast regular glances to her left and right as she paced forward. In this manner she saw me. I fired as soon as she rotated her numismatic profile. She staggered and fell. The sound of my gunshot almost obscured hers. I had, by sheer chance, struck her squarely in the chest. Her blood, i.e., pearly darkness: well, it appeared. She tried to sit up and failed, proof that my own insult had worked on her. I had so successfully crushed and insulted her that she could not sit up. Because I did not want to walk all the way back to the place I'd left Klemperer, I did not use my shovel this time. I used the butt of her gun. It lay next to another clump of cinquefoil turning its leaves up in a minor breeze.

She shit herself when her forehead caved in. The smell mingled with the smells of the grass, the air, the sunlight, my own sweat, her blood, my blood, Klemperer's blood, the earth. The crushed and insulted can behave in whatever manner they choose, assuming they have a choice. If they have no choice, this iron and mustache-like law still stands. Therefore the soul exists. No thanks to the great defecator, God. Amen.

15.

AHEAD OF ME, FLOATING in the dimness, a stripe of raw-looking flesh. It belonged to no one, no one at all.

Instead, I decided to observe the meat truck that had been driving next to me almost since I left the field near Cañuelas. The driver smiled through his window. I returned the smile through mine. He mistook me, I think, for a Departmental officer. I was wearing Klemperer's uniform and over it the sky-blue windbreaker I found folded into a dense, loud oblong beneath the passenger seat. The windbreaker hid the blood speckling its collar and epaulettes and concealed, as well, the widening, continental stain my own blood was leaving on the cloth. I'd shoved Luxemburg's undershirt against the wound. I didn't know if Ojea's drivers had to obey a protocol regarding Departmental officers. This driver, my driver, seemed intent on screening me from traffic, and thus from threats. Possibly he was obeying; possibly he was concerned about my fate. The huge blue words on the side panel vibrated along with the nonexistent carbuncles. I was concerned at first that these visual phenomena would interfere with my ability to drive, but they did not.

Violeta's admonition about the airport closure concerned me. Or rather it concerned Pasternak. I myself felt only a mild eddy, a mild disturbance. Besides, it was almost sunset now, almost dusk. Had I slept, after dragging myself into the driver's seat? In any case, time was lost, no matter how or how much. Other people seemed to be heading for the airport, taxis streamed toward the same off-ramp I took. When we pulled into the complex of overpasses and access roads around Pistarini, it was clear the airport was fully operational. Indeed, there was not even any residual traffic or congestion. I reached the long-term lot without difficulty (except for a few more sprays of pink foam from my mouth, because I'd started to cough). There was a line, but a normal one, and it made no difference because the parking attendants waved me ahead of the cars waiting. No one objected, I watched in the rearview mirror for rebellion among the drivers and passengers I was defrauding, but their faces remained set, still, uniform. The roofed lot smelled like gasoline. Lackeys in sky-blue coveralls, like the one I had seen effacing Ana's name from her office door, carried red cans into a dark doorway near where I parked. I stepped down from the van. They averted their eyes from my passage. Luxemburg's undershirt was warm and tacky against my skin, dense now with my own blood. The parking lot elevator stank of gasoline more strongly than the lot itself. A lackey had spilled fuel here and said nothing. Silence being the number one weapon of lackeys.

On a high walkway inside the main terminal, I watched through a window a detachment of my fellow officers (so to speak) marching out past the runways to the fen-like waste fields that surrounded Pistarini. The air I inhaled still cold and still sweet. I counted four officers, three women and one man, all carrying shovels. They reached a far point out in the field and set to work, their shovels glinting in the sunlight. They dug and they dug. Gray earth flew in spurts. The hole, rectilinear, deepened, grew darker, a void in the bright day. They stopped work. Their mouths moved in laughter. One, a woman, planted her shovel blade in the ground. From this ground, it seemed, some tender, some human curl was arising, black and dense. Above the digging officers, planes angled earthward. On the north terminal wall, a sky-blue banner hung. From ceiling to floor. It too trembled in the ceaseless, invisible breeze. Sketched on it in outline the features of Sanchis Mira. Mustache, necktie. His large hands at rest on a closed book. All the porteños in the airport ignored the banner; all the tourists pointed at it and murmured, assuring each other that it was a statesman, an Argentine statesman long dead. One even guessed it was Pistarini himself. It must be, he muttered, or why would they hang it so prominently? The tourists did not avert their eyes from mine as I passed among them, but the porteños did.

I first stumbled near the men's room entrance. A lackey in a coverall was mopping the floor. I caught myself against the jamb. The lackey plunged his mop into the bucket on gray wheels that he would push through the airport and then through eternity. I muttered to him: Be more careful where you splash that water, you fucking faggot. He started mopping again as soon as I finished speaking, he wheeled the bucket away. The axles whined. In the men's room, I unzipped my windbreaker. The right side of Klemperer's shirt, hip to armpit, was bloodstained. I unbuttoned it to examine the wound. I pressed the flesh around the neat, dense hole. No pain, just lightness. The male officer with the shovel barged into the bathroom just as I finished zipping the windbreaker closed again over my hastily buttoned shirt. The shovel's dented head carried crusts of gray earth. One crust tumbled to the white floor and shattered. The noise pure and thunderous, like the initial rumor of a storm. The stall door slammed. The officer started to grunt. I swallowed the blood and bile filling my mouth.

A few droplets, a few ovate droplets. I couldn't avoid leaving them behind me as I crossed the terminal. I felt them slide down my arm, down my hand, and before I could close my fist and smear them away, they fell from my fingertips. Always some effluvium, Pasternak. Or even refulgence. I was lighter and lighter, lighter with every step. Fortunate, because it allowed me to continue, and unfortunate because the world grew heavier and heavier, so heavy that even the glances of passersby and tourists weighed me down. Someone kept demanding someone else over the announcement system. Would a Mr. Sordini (or Sortini, I couldn't tell) please report to the courtesy lounge. In Spanish, in English. A white roaring, too, underlay the words. A sea, the hidden sea. I walked, I floated, so to speak, behind a couple with matching haircuts and suitcases.

They ended up in front of me in the line for international departures. They were bound for Portland, a city the ticket agent had never heard of. The couple seemed surprised, they regarded Portland as a western capital. All three laughed at this, loudly and frankly; all three stopped laughing in the same breath and stiffened. The ticket agent directed a shy, defeated glance my way. I dipped my head in salute, leaning on the silver poles connected by moire nylon ribbons, sky blue. The couple hauled their matching strawberry-covered luggage toward the gate entrances, and the red, achene-pricked forms continued to burn among the carbuncles, stars, and assholes.

In the back pocket of Klemperer's pants was his wallet. I planned to use his credit card—issued by the University's own bank and the same sky blue as the departmental uniform—but had no idea of its limit, or if the authorities were aware of his death and had alerted banks and other commercial bodies to watch out for transactions made in his name. If this plan failed … yet it didn't matter. The ticket agent was nodding me forward. I swallowed another copious mouthful of my own blood and obeyed. But the swallowing, this time, made me cough. The red streak my cough painted across the agent's round, whitening face resembled, I thought, my friend's letter *L* in minuscule.

But my head was now bouncing mildly against the cool floor tiles. I coughed up another vivid chevron of blood. Shoes and ankles darted and dodged across my visual field, among the reddish occurrences. Primate voices cried out above me. I could no longer distinguish the words. The beating of my heart, sevenfold, seventyfold. Questions arose. Was this death, "Pasternak" wanted to know. Pasternak murmured and whimpered. And I myself? Well, I had nothing to say.

16.

GRASS-BLADES PENETRATED SO DEEPLY into my nostrils that I leapt up in terror. They carried the scents of: dust, dandelion pollen, loam, and human corpses. Also marble, the rubber soles of shoes, rainwater.

I leapt up and fell back on my side at once, simply because the movement I attempted—to "leap to my feet"—failed. True, my legs locked and prepared to support my thorax and head, but my back would not straighten. The sunset blinded me, so I tumbled back to the grass. I tried to cry out. A desert dryness consumed and degraded the sound.

I tried again to spread my palms on the grass and force myself at least to my knees, and this worked, though I was not on my knees; I was "standing," a bodily voice whispered. My head and chest pointed forward and my abdomen pointed earthward, my genitals (to my amazement naked) swaying ponderously in the warm breeze. The need to urinate stung my bladder (my soul) and my right leg rose, without effort, from the grassy earth. The urine streamed and sputtered, I heard it, but I could not see it, and my burgherly training seized hold, crept over and crawled over, shouting that I must stop pissing, at once, at once, but I could not stop, I trotted in a tight circle attempting to see my own urination, and my right leg, it is true, participated, but I could not see it, I could not see it, and it ended before I asserted myself over the secret strength of my bladder (again: my soul).

Pistarini: gone. As if consumed by mighty, motionless fire. And the endless white tiles, these were gone as well. No thicket of pampas grasses enclosed the lawn I was trotting in mindless circles around. Klemperer and Luxemburg? The invisible fire had taken them, too. Their absence prompted me to fill my lungs and shout. This time, a cry did emerge, a single, curt, meaningless, fluid monosyllable. To my east, my west, my north, and my south, monuments. Gray marble, white marble, concrete. Cruciform. Some stood at the heads of brick borders demarcating oblong plots, some stood in naked grass, and some on raw earth. Among them larger constructions, spires and plinths, and even (occupying double or triple the land) white and gray stone mausolea. The setting sun visible over the brown wall, not far but not near, like the mouth of a furnace. Or even an eye, Pasternak, don't forget you can always compare the sun to an eye. In the nothing that flowed between the monuments, the nothing the monuments combed, comb of the so-called hecatomb, dozens of dogs were waking up. They followed the same protocol. They stood, they pissed or even shat, they circled their own axis, and they began to trot southwest, toward Warnes, I realized. Where the gap in the cemetery wall was. These dogs ignored me, as they had during my long excursion among them on my first night in the southern capital. As they passed, their muzzles stayed on the same level as my own face, and their blank, mildly phosphorescent gazes met mine. As the first dog approached me, an obese rottweiler with foamy ropes of saliva dangling from her jowls, I panicked, yes, Pasternak panicked and tried again to rise up, to assume the primate stance of supremacy. I fell once more onto my flank, and the rottweiler let her glance slide over me as I struggled in the damp grass.

I knew where I was. La Chacarita. More dogs rushed between the gravestones, more dogs slipped past me. I lay there, and I attempted to cry. I felt no sadness, I felt nothing at all. But one "ought" to cry over such abrupt transformations. Yes, yes, because of my intelligence (and please recall its true definition) I knew what had happened. The sole possible outcome. A great loss, an irreplaceable loss, all cultural authorities tell us. We humans stand atop the world, the world exists only as our extension, in fact as our extended extensiveness. And now, this loss. So I tried to cry, I failed. Weeping is forbidden to dogs.

The others, my new colleagues, well, they didn't care that I was just lying around doing nothing. They trotted on past me over the tall, rich grass. The worst was that Fulvio had been correct. He refuted me from the beginning, and pedants suffer refutation as pure torment. Still no weeping, not even a dry, forced sob. I was panting, drooling; my nose snuffled up the mingled and maximal scents the graveyard earth supplied. My colleagues had no difficulty walking. I could not be the only new one, I could not be the only man who had died in Buenos Aires the previous day. So get the fuck up, Pasternak, I thought, get the fuck up.

I got "up." I walked. On four legs, on my "arms" and my legs, my fore- and hind legs. My "hands" and my "feet" spread at each step against the cooling grass. It took no real effort, my limbs knew what to do, and they bore me along among the other dogs, quiet and direct. I could not believe my fate, yet it had descended. That's the trouble with fate, it descends. The need to shit seized my bowels (my soul) as the need to piss had seized my bladder, and I stopped to squat and defecate, my legs searching out the correct, most sturdy position. The dogs still trooped past me as two, then three hot turds slid from my asshole. What pleasure, to defecate in ease and security, no straining or meditative life allowed, merely to shit and to leave the shit behind you as progress toward the gap in the wall. Through which the sun glares above the toothed roofline. As the glowing, pink sky floated along above me, I recalled my days of higher stature. But so what? Those days had ended, as surely as my transformation had sealed the wound in my side. And I'd never been this at ease among humans—never, not once. Though by definition this anxiety would have remained hidden during my human life. Yes, I felt at ease among my new colleagues, even eager. No querulous doubts, no endless speculations. Speculations lie rooted in envy. Pasternak = dog. Dogs possess no envy. QED. I pushed through the press of my colleagues at the hole and crossed the railroad tracks on Warnes. They didn't speak and they didn't interfere. More than I can say for my academic colleagues, more than I could have said for any other human. The dogs were running. Which is to say, Pasternak, that we were running, we, we, we. And no one else. We ran and ran, the cooling pavement touched the rubbery, sensitive pads of our feet, of my feet. Night breezes curled into our ears, along our backs. All around me, beneath raised tails, assholes rubious or black, and the greener, yellower blackness of the city night. Now I smelled meat, now saliva poured down my throat, fell from my bouncing jaws, now I smelled the incomparable smell of clean tap water in a clean bowl.

The city spread before us. A bit higher and a bit darker than before. One thing I can say about the claim that dogs are color-blind is that it is a lie: I saw color with an intense and perfected fervor, every tawny stick, every bluish seam in the pavement, every coagulated brick, every pore in every limestone plinth. But the city spread and spread, its streets locked in place. The same city, the same Buenos Aires. Even the same approaching night. I passed the bench I slept on during my first excursion. Now some bird shit, which I could smell, streaked the marble. Grayish-black, with a grave crimson speck in the center. But this bird shit could not hold my attention. I saw Adriano leaning on the wooden counter of his stand. Hilário sat on a wooden crate. They were both smoking and looking at the stream of dogs pouring through the entrance plaza. I stopped, I broke away from the pack and moved toward them.

As soon as they noticed me heading their way a stony and simultaneous blankness stiffened their faces. I "called" to them—Adriano! Hilário!—before I could overcome the urge. I said nothing, of course. I just let out three bright, tenor barks and kept on running toward them. I'd almost reached the stand when Hilário rose and Adriano reached under the counter and lifted an aluminum baseball bat. Get the fuck out of here, you worthless motherfucker, he hissed, and darted through the entrance flap in the blue tarpaulin side wall. Hilário said nothing; he took a long step toward me, wound up, and aimed a strong, looping kick at my flank. The blow missed. The breeze from his shoe touched my pelt. There was a gray-pink gobbet of gum stuck to the treads. I smelled its unbearable sweetness. Get out! Get out! Adriano went on screaming, getting closer and closer and adjusting his grip on the bat handle. I only noticed as I was skittering away that Fulvio's stand was gone, that Adriano was out there alone on the marble pavement.

But I had no time to ponder Fulvio's absence. The uncle and nephew went on cursing me long after I had rejoined the pack.

You motherfucker! Motherfucker! tore through and through the soft night. Hilário even picked up a stone and hurled it at me, but it scraped along the sidewalk and took a bad bounce, ending up in the gutter. The smells of meat and clean water became overpowering, and I rushed along with all my other colleagues, nameless and fleet, to the bowls. Yes, the bowls! How hard to communicate the joy and satisfaction they produced. While a human would have failed miserably under such circumstances, hesitating and hobbling, terrified of being elbowed or yelled at, I ate, I drank, no one prevented me from taking my share, I just stuck my head down and chewed at the meat piled up by the more dutiful residents, and I lapped the same water my colleagues lapped, tasting their saliva, too. We flowed along as a single stream and we ate, we drank, we left no bowl empty. With one exception: none of us had eaten or drunk from a bowl set out in front of a furniture store, Ophuls Home and Garden. The display window expressed a certain sweet and cold melancholy. In it a luminescent bathtub on four clawed legs cowered before a naked mannequin about to dip its blunt, cuneal foot past the white rim. The meat in the bowl was also luminescent, and odorous. The water cloudy. Not as bad as the meat in the bowl at the all-night store. And no sad-eyed clerk to be seen.

You are awake, Pasternak, and you are alive. And while no one is left in this unpredictable life to call you Boris Leonidovich, so you remain. Far from the prisons of the Mongolians, far from the Butyrka, and far from the carcel. Hunger twisted my bowels and more saliva leapt into my long mouth, beneath my thick, pink tongue. Each time I opened it to breathe a husky pant emerged. Warnes passed into darkness ahead of me. The old orphanage west of Punta Arenas lay concealed on its wooded plot to my north. My tail trembled in the warming wind. My goal lay ahead of me, far ahead, and the danger of death and capture beset my way. Yet I did not presume and I did not despair. I was no longer human.

17.

THE ONLY REAL CONCERN facing dogs is the need to go on existing. Although this does not make them afraid of death. It is not the same as the human need for life, which is abstract and proleptic. No, a dog needs only to go on existing for a day, an hour, an instant, that's all. If death comes in the next instant, it does not matter to him. To fear death, to notice death means you are a slave, a human slave (a pleonasm). Ana's death, my own death, of these take no note. Death holds terrors only if you live, and dogs do not live. As noted, a dog merely exists. And to exist is to enjoy an ontological purity humans can never attain.

Perhaps the strongest proof of this is the ease with which I accepted my new condition. Apart from the few moments of theatrical and specious internal sorrow over my alleged loss, I had not experienced a single doubt, a single quiver of fear. Since leaving the cemetery I only gained confidence and calm with every step, darting to any meat or water bowl I chose and boldly, brazenly lowering my muzzle. The sight of my reflection in the water made me happy and proud. Look at those bright eyes, look at that healthy tongue and the mighty depths of the nostrils. My god, the apelike mask you once wore. But there was not even the "apelike mask." A dog has no use for metaphors; metaphors are lies and as such are wholly and eternally foreign to the animal kingdom. This confidence gave me the courage to ignore, as well, the few strangers I saw abroad, to brush past them as I walked and feel no more human need to excuse myself, to apologize for the fact of my occupying space.

Better still, I had no obligation to anyone, to any place, any instant. I could turn aside from my path whenever I wished and adopt an entirely new route. Going along one street did not tether me to that street; passing a turnoff did not foreclose on that turnoff. A ceaseless and mindless improvisation, without the sickening awareness of improvising that improvising itself creates. Action followed action, event followed event. I paced along, and the calm moon came out. I lapped at a bowl, and a newscaster shouted from a radio. Some corpuscles slipped through my heart and lungs. The tall, rust-spotted crimson mailbox I was at rest behind cooled my neck. The human in the gray cloth jacket walking toward me as if in a dream stopped when I slipped out from behind the mailbox and sauntered past him toward Camacuá. Around us, the drilling whines of mosquitoes passed through the damp air like current.

I had no evil intent but the human regarded me with surprise all the same, and I wondered if he was another traveler, another visitor to the pension. This brief encounter took place between two lakes of pure night on a pavement gleaming in places with rain. I smelled the heartbreaking scent of wet pavement, first, and the dragged scent, the smeared scent shod feet leave behind, as well as urine, which electrified me, and feces, a contemplative scent, dust (which smells the way moonlight looks) and the fragrances of combustion, ozone, and burning esters.

The footsteps of the jacket-wearing human faded in the distance, beyond the last penumbra of streetlamp light. From

Thorne I passed to Curapaligüé, from Curapaligüé to Puma-cahua, Carabobo, and Lautaro. The pavement was giving off warmth and the meat bowls, which shone in semiregular lines extending along either curb, were piled with meat. I knew precisely what this meat was. But the meat quivered in the bowls, and I quivered in answer. I lowered my blunt muzzle to the meat and chewed as my saliva spurted and my hind paws scraped the sidewalk. The meat was fresh, strong smelling, and fibrous. Each water bowl I lapped from showed me my blunted face, my night-colored fur, my yellowed eyes. I listened for the whistles and drumbeats trailing from radios, and I interrupted my meal to scan Bonifacio for MAN'S BEST FRIEND SOCIETY vans, but without fear, without even any "interest," to use the human phrase. I did not see one, not one, not a single van. Though absence proves nothing to a dog.

Before I reached Camacuá, I smelled them: Macedonias. The empty night carried their scent to me. Hard and perceptible as cement, for example, or as the limestone steps gleaming in the jaundiced light five yards, six yards ahead. I paused to observe these steps. A poplar's bent shadow lay across them, and above them the coal of a cigarette glowed. At the top, where the tree shadow ended, sat Violeta. She had not noticed me yet; she sat with her knees raised and her arms on her knees, her hair re-strained by an amethyst band. I trotted forward and my nails tapped the sidewalk. That Violeta heard me approach I knew, though she did not turn her head. Her eyes, the whites and the dark pupils, slid wetly, that's all. Her meat bowl full. A white blot afloat on the surface of the water in the water bowl: the streetlamp in reflection. This image shattered as I plunged my muzzle in.

Two colleagues passed by, a pug and a Labrador, both shuffling along with their muzzles close to the cooling sidewalk. The Labrador sank (as a joke) his canines into the rugose pelt covering the short neck of the pug, a vague pinkish-gray like worn wallpaper. The pug danced away and snapped his own jaws shut, but his asthmatic breathing destroyed the effect. Both dogs ignored Violeta and me, and she did not look at them, she kept her dark gaze on my dark fur, watching me as I ate. The meat slabs in her bowl were cold, slightly stiff. This made them harder to chew but it masked their flavor. The minuscule, wet noise her bowed lips made as they left the cigarette butt accompanied my vigorous chewing. I finished eating, I drank again, I inhaled some smoke that was drifting my way, and I scraped at my muzzle with my left forepaw. (Curiously, my metempsychosis had changed my dominant "hand.")

I looked up at my former hostess expecting nothing and I received nothing. She stared into my eyes. Were it not for my inability to speak, I could have conveyed my true being. I am Pasternak, despite this form, I am Pasternak, your former client and guest. Though I was not Pasternak, I was a dog, a black bullmastiff, broad in the shoulder and chest as I had been during human life, with a blunt face and one torn ear, weighing (I estimated) sixty pounds. Violeta ground out her cigarette and returned to the parlor, and I ate the last red fragments from the bowl. My legs wanted to go on, but I was at the mercy of no one and nothing, not even my legs, so instead I trotted around the side of the pension to the wooden garden gate, which I saw was ajar. Beyond, leafy darkness. I pushed it open with my muzzle and my left paw. On the other side, two ceramic roosters, both sky blue, stood guard.

From the garden, you could see into the back parlor. (I was reclining near her lush tomato patch, amid the strong, narcotic smell of their vines and leaves.) Six strangers gathered there, in the lacquerous light. They had Northern European accents; Danish, I thought, because their heads had the square, nobly stupid quality Danish skulls possess (shaped by the wind, the sea, and other such healthy elemental phenomena). The Spanish they spoke, while technically sound, flowed from their mouths in the accents of a stone fish. Their voices, stiffened by burgherly excitement, floated out above me in the warm darkness. Violeta was explaining to them, as she had once to me, that she did not understand the origin of the night dogs, but that she herself had never been affected by them adversely. I hope they will not lower your opinion of our city, she added. The guests all chimed in to assure her that such a thing would never occur, that in Copenhagen (had I been a human, this confirmation of my theory would have gratified me, as a dog I felt nothing, nothing at all) dogs also ran wild at night. It was a new phenomenon, said a female guest, but we have all gotten used to it and indeed would not know what to do in a city where dogs did not occupy the streets after sunset. But here, added a man, here it is like something from a story, whereas at home we could not say that. No, no, said the female guest, it is nothing like a story, you cannot compare real life to a story. Violeta's face I could not see. She had turned her back to the window. Light poured through her thin shirt, revealing her dark, ample, erect body.

The man had spoken loudly. His North Sea voice echoed through the dark garden. An embarrassed silence rose among the guests. Violeta filled it by observing that she had to go begin her nightly struggle to sleep. She pointed out three wine bottles on the sideboard and informed the guests that they were welcome to drink them, as she could not due to her barbiturate consumption. Soon, in her bedroom, the lights came on. I looked upward. She was undressing, removing her white shirt and purple lace brassiere, freeing her heavy, lightly deflated breasts, the left much larger than the right, the areolas broad and dark. In the flesh beneath them a red dent from the brassiere's wire. She concealed these philosophical breasts again beneath a green T-shirt with a white logo across it: JUMBO. Her window was open, so as the guests fell into vinous silence I listened for her voice. Inner instinct pricked me, alerting me that she would soon begin to speak, and she did. It was clear that she was speaking into a telephone. She was asking for the twenty-four-hour service line, waiting, repeating her request, and thanking the operator. She then explained that she had a problem she wanted to report. At that point she moved away from the window and I lost her voice. As a merely existent being, I did not concern myself with this.

The parlor activities went on and on. The Danes opened and closed their teeth in a hidden and sublime order, one I could not despite my generally improved senses detect. They talked about further plans for the trip, the cultural and aesthetic "events" that lay ahead. As if forming a swamp. We really must get out to Mendoza, said the woman, and marine laughter broke forth once more, though she had not said anything amusing. I rose and stretched my limbs as I prepared to canter between the blue roosters and back out onto José Bonifacio. But a noise, a mechanical sound—the indignant noise a van engine makes as it spins down—gave me pause. The chalky beam of a flashlight flashed across the garden fence.

I held my breath. Above the fence a sky-blue hat cruised along, then stopped. The garden gate sang as it was pushed fully open. Between the two sky-blue roosters I observed two sky-blue legs. The ovoid of glare from the flashlight traveled across the brick path. The legs belonged to an officer I did not recognize. He was young, thin, and short; he had the face of a mole, puffy and blind. His baton hung at his left side, his pistol at his left. On his upper lip a faint reddish down sprouted. He gave a soft whistle and called out: Here, boy. I looked up at Violeta's window again, expecting her to be standing against it and watching, but she was gone, the window was dark, and the Danish guests were laughing their nasal, watery laughs. The officer approached the tomato patch and moved the light across it. I had forgotten to shut my eyes, and he must have seen them flashing green or yellow, because he muttered to himself: There you are, boy, come on, boy. He was carrying in his free hand a pink slab of meat, which he waved back and forth. The meat was almost the same shade as his fat, light-coated cheeks.

At last, I thought. As if I had been awaiting this tentative and clumsy young man. He did not smell me, but I smelled him, his sweat, the rum on his breath. Decaying teeth as well. The detergent in his uniform and the polish on his high boots. I backed up, closer to the tomato vines and hedges to hide myself. Their cool shadow embraced me, sleeved my pelt. The young officer lost track of me. I saw it in his eyes when I glanced up (now I kept my face aimed earthward as he swung the flashlight back and forth). It was much easier to evade these agents, these state breathers, as a dog. I remembered without rancor or self-pity all the difficulties his now-dead colleagues had caused me, all the pain they had inflicted. True. Nevertheless—well, for one human to kill another, that belongs to the moral world. For a human to kill a dog, that does too. But the moral world excludes whatever does not originate with humanity.

The cupped leaves of the tomato vines held darkness. The windows of the Pensión Vermesser held light. The young officer struggling to grow a mustache came closer, still looking for me. The glow from the window crossed the nameplate on his sky-blue chest: SCHULZ. I recalled the stiff cloth of Klemperer's uniform against my human shoulders. Officer Schulz came closer and closer, his voice growing louder and lighter at each step, as though he were speaking to a child. Finally his cries alerted the Danish guests in the back parlor. They set down their wine glasses and came to the window; one of them asked Schulz what he was looking for, and he answered, without any shame: A dog, the owner called; you have no idea the trouble they cause law-abiding citizens and business owners. I glanced up toward Violeta's window. She was there again, in her green shirt, staring down, her mouth impassive and her eyes half-closed.

As Schulz gave this little speech, the meat still flapped in his hand. Back and forth, back and forth. That I could smell, too, and the blood trickling from it down his wrist and into the uniform cloth. In his van, a service radio began to hiss and chime. His words, dull as they were, calmed the guests. The woman made no more objections. She leaned on the sill, looking from Schulz to the darkness where she imagined I was. Schulzpor was already twisting his boy's mouth—the presence of this woman added a new audience for him. I gazed between the vines at the young officer. Through his veins, pearly darkness pulsed, I knew, and pearly darkness craves its source. The night lay in curved sections along the streets. The streets retreated, eternally. My course became clear. Saliva filled the hollow beneath my tongue and poured over my pointed teeth. In the moment of bodily unguardedness that precedes action, my bladder spasmed and my urine sprayed the grass. The modest noise made Schulz widen his false smile. He saw me now, he waved the meat, he flapped his right hand to summon me closer. An artery jumped under the hinge of his jaw near the skin. I set my feet, tensed my muscles, I prepared to leap. And I realized I could, for the first time, smell the sea.

New Directions Paperbooks — a partial listing

César Aira, Ema, the Captive
An Episode in the Life of a Landscape Painter
Ghosts
Will Alexander, The Sri Lankan Loxodrome
Osama Alomar, The Teeth of the Comb
Guillaume Apollinaire, Selected Writings
Paul Auster, The Red Notebook
Honoré de Balzac, Colonel Chabert
Djuna Barnes, Nightwood
Jorge Barón Biza, The Desert and Its Seed
Charles Baudelaire, The Flowers of Evil*
Bei Dao, City Gate, Open Up
Nina Berberova, The Ladies From St. Petersburg
Mei-Mei Berssenbrugge, Hello, the Roses
Max Blecher, Adventures in Immediate Irreality
Roberto Bolaño, By Night in Chile
Distant Star
Nazi Literature in the Americas
Jorge Luis Borges, Labyrinths
Seven Nights
Coral Bracho, Firefly Under the Tongue*
Kamau Brathwaite, Ancestors
Basil Bunting, Complete Poems
Anne Carson, Antigonick
Glass, Irony & God
Horacio Castellanos Moya, Senselessness
Camilo José Cela, Mazurka for Two Dead Men
Louis-Ferdinand Céline
Death on the Installment Plan
Journey to the End of the Night
Rafael Chirbes, On the Edge
Inger Christensen, alphabet
Jean Cocteau, The Holy Terrors
Julio Cortázar, Cronopios & Famas
62: A Model Kit
Robert Creeley, If I Were Writing This
Guy Davenport, 7 Greeks
Osamu Dazai, No Longer Human
H. D., Selected Poems
Tribute to Freud
Helen DeWitt, The Last Samurai
Daša Drndić, Belladonna
Robert Duncan, Selected Poems
Eça de Queirós, The Illustrious House of Ramires
William Empson, 7 Types of Ambiguity
Mathias Énard, Compass
Shusaku Endo, Deep River

Jenny Erpenbeck, The End of Days
Go, Went, Gone
Visitation
Lawrence Ferlinghetti
A Coney Island of the Mind
F. Scott Fitzgerald, The Crack-Up
On Booze
Forrest Gander, The Trace
Romain Gary, Promise at Dawn
Henry Green, Concluding
John Hawkes, Travesty
Felisberto Hernández, Piano Stories
Hermann Hesse, Siddhartha
Takashi Hiraide, The Guest Cat
Yoel Hoffmann, Moods
Susan Howe, My Emily Dickinson
Debths
Bohumil Hrabal, I Served the King of England
Qurratulain Hyder, River of Fire
Sonallah Ibrahim, That Smell
Rachel Ingalls, Mrs. Caliban
Christopher Isherwood, The Berlin Stories
Fleur Jaeggy, I Am the Brother of XX
Alfred Jarry, Ubu Roi
B. S. Johnson, House Mother Normal
James Joyce, Stephen Hero
Franz Kafka, Amerika: The Man Who Disappeared
Investigations of a Dog
Yasunari Kawabata, Dandelions
John Keene, Counternarratives
Alexander Kluge, Temple of the Scapegoat
Laszlo Krasznahorkai, Satantango
Seiobo There Below
War and War
Ryszard Krynicki, Magnetic Point
Eka Kurniawan, Beauty Is a Wound
Mme. de Lafayette, The Princess of Clèves
Lautréamont, Maldoror
Denise Levertov, Selected Poems
Li Po, Selected Poems
Clarice Lispector, The Hour of the Star
Near to the Wild Heart
The Passion According to G. H.
Federico García Lorca, Selected Poems*
Three Tragedies
Nathaniel Mackey, Splay Anthem
Xavier de Maistre, Voyage Around My Room
Stéphane Mallarmé, Selected Poetry and Prose*

Javier Marías, Your Face Tomorrow (3 volumes)
Harry Mathews, The Solitary Twin
Bernadette Mayer, Works & Days
Carson McCullers, The Member of the Wedding
Thomas Merton, New Seeds of Contemplation
The Way of Chuang Tzu
Henri Michaux, A Barbarian in Asia
Dunya Mikhail, The Beekeeper
Henry Miller, The Colossus of Maroussi
Big Sur & the Oranges of Hieronymus Bosch
Yukio Mishima, Confessions of a Mask
Death in Midsummer
Eugenio Montale, Selected Poems*
Vladimir Nabokov, Laughter in the Dark
Nikolai Gogol
The Real Life of Sebastian Knight
Raduan Nassar, A Cup of Rage
Pablo Neruda, The Captain's Verses*
Love Poems*
Residence on
Charles Olson, Selected Writings
George Oppen, New Collected Poems
Wilfred Owen, Collected Poems
Michael Palmer, The Laughter of the Sphinx
Nicanor Parra, Antipoems*
Boris Pasternak, Safe Conduct
Kenneth Patchen
Memoirs of a Shy Pornographer
Octavio Paz, Poems of Octavio Paz
Victor Pelevin, Omon Ra
Alejandra Pizarnik
Extracting the Stone of Madness
Ezra Pound, The Cantos
New Selected Poems and Translations
Raymond Queneau, Exercises in Style
Qian Zhongshu, Fortress Besieged
Raja Rao, Kanthapura
Herbert Read, The Green Child
Kenneth Rexroth, Selected Poems
Keith Ridgway, Hawthorn & Child
Rainer Maria Rilke
Poems from the Book of Hours
Arthur Rimbaud, Illuminations*
A Season in Hell and The Drunken Boat*
Guillermo Rosales, The Halfway House
Evelio Rosero, The Armies
Fran Ross, Oreo
Joseph Roth, The Emperor's Tomb
The Hotel Years

Raymond Roussel, Locus Solus
Ihara Saikaku, The Life of an Amorous Woman
Nathalie Sarraute, Tropisms
Jean-Paul Sartre, Nausea
The Wall
Delmore Schwartz
In Dreams Begin Responsibilities
Hasan Shah, The Dancing Girl
W. G. Sebald, The Emigrants
The Rings of Saturn
Vertigo
Stevie Smith, Best Poems
Gary Snyder, Turtle Island
Muriel Spark, The Driver's Seat
The Girls of Slender Means
Memento Mori
Reiner Stach, Is That Kafka?
Antonio Tabucchi, Pereira Maintains
Junichiro Tanizaki, A Cat, a Man & Two Women
Yoko Tawada, The Emissary
Memoirs of a Polar Bear
Dylan Thomas, A Child's Christmas in Wales
Collected Poems
Uwe Timm, The Invention of Curried Sausage
Tomas Tranströmer
The Great Enigma: New Collected Poems
Leonid Tsypkin, Summer in Baden-Baden
Tu Fu, Selected Poems
Frederic Tuten, The Adventures of Mao
Regina Ullmann, The Country Road
Paul Valéry, Selected Writings
Enrique Vila-Matas, Bartleby & Co.
Vampire in Love
Elio Vittorini, Conversations in Sicily
Rosmarie Waldrop, Gap Gardening
Robert Walser, The Assistant
Microscripts
The Tanners
Eliot Weinberger, The Ghosts of Birds
Nathanael West, The Day of the Locust
Miss Lonelyhearts
Tennessee Williams, Cat on a Hot Tin Roof
The Glass Menagerie
A Streetcar Named Desire
William Carlos Williams, Selected Poems
Spring and All
Mushtaq Ahmed Yousufi, Mirages of the Mind
Louis Zukofsky, "A"
Anew

*BILINGUAL EDITION

For a complete listing, request a free catalog from New Directions, 80 8th Avenue, New York, NY 10011
or visit us online at ndbooks.com